Echoes of Austin

Garrick Blake

Preface

The dreams always start the same way.

I'm on a quiet cul-de-sac, looking at the front of a comfortably worn house. Walking up the front steps, I can't help but look up at the bead-board ceiling over the small front porch. It's covered in spiderwebs and abandoned wasp nests. I can't even tell what color it used to be. I turn the knob and push the heavy wooden door. This puts me in a fairly modern, split-level house.

To the right, an apartment over the garage sports a spare bedroom and a weird, white chaise lounge that came with the house.

To the left, a dark hallway with multiple exits begins with a guest bathroom on the left, which is perpetually just a bit sticky. I know—I had replaced the tile to no effect.

I stumble exhaustedly through the living room and into the dining room and pour a drink. To my left, dark shapes cavort in my peripheral vision. I ignore them. It takes effort.

Shadow people, apparitions, missing items, electrical fires. The logical explanation is I'm going insane.

I pour another drink before the ice from my first is gone.

I face the corner. I can't see the shapes anymore, but now I can hear them—laughing at me. They know I can't stop them. I don't have any control over the house I own or the ability to help the family I am supposed to protect.

And I know that's true.

Ignoring it is the only way to keep going. Every bit of effort is required.

As I pour my third drink, it takes less.

Chapter One

As the old Scottish prayer says, the night is dark and filled with ghoulies and ghosties and long-legged beasties and things that go bump in the night. Everyone knows that.

What you eventually learn is that it is generally safer to try to limit your contact to those long-legged beasties that you've bought drinks for. Knowing this and sticking to it have always been two very separate things for me. This is why I was dragging myself on my back through a dark attic in the middle of a Georgia summer, with every inch of progress met with what felt like a pound of powdery insulation accumulating in the back of my jeans.

New construction attics are always full of this intrusive insulation. It's great for the energy bills but terrible if you don't want your pants full of gray wads of fiber.

I dug around behind and under my head until I felt the drywall ceiling and knocked. "Did you hear it here?" I yelled towards the attic opening.

"Hang on," I heard from the hallway under me. "Knock again."

I did.

"Closer to the wall, I think," came the uncertain reply.

I sighed and grabbed another rafter, and pulled myself forward, forcing a fresh load of insulation into my pants. I knocked again. "Here?"

"Yeah, that's where I hear the footsteps."

I pulled my phone out of my pocket and used the feeble screen light to get a better look. A patch of the insulation was discolored. When I touched it, the cold made it almost feel damp. It would have been a nice change from the sweltering attic if it didn't smell like rot and dirt.

I set my phone on a cross beam and let the screen light up the plywood underside of the roof. I fished an Electric and Magnetic Field detector out of my pocket and popped in a fresh battery.

I switched it on and set it next to the phone, LEDs dark.

Until science bothers to create an actual ghost detector, the closest we can get is detecting weak electrical fields that can mean something is attempting to manifest nearby. Of course, it can also mean you need a new toaster. The EMF detector is a vital component in my limited toolbox.

Tapping the phone screen left the attic filled with long shadows cast by the indirect light from the open entry hatch. I closed my eyes and settled in to wait.

"Come on," I muttered into the darkness, "Do your thing."

I heard a faint scampering overhead. No doubt, a squirrel was taking a shortcut across the roof to get between some of the pine trees the builders had left in place.

Aside from the heat and the sweat soaking the collar of my shirt, the board digging into my spine, and the threat of something really, really nasty I don't know about sharing the dark with me, this was my favorite part of the job. If you've seen one dark attic, I won't suggest you've seen them all, but holy shit, you've seen most of them.

A dark attic with reported ghostly activity is an adventure. In this case, an adventure that was going to make me late getting my rental car returned.

THUMP

"There we go!" I looked over at the EMF detector and watched the lights blink green, steady but not quickly.

THUMP THUMP

The lights flashed from yellow to red, increasing in speed before settling on solid red.

"If you don't have anything to do but stomp around, I'm done here," I promised.

Nothing.

Typical.

"Toss me my bag?" I called towards the attic stairs. A few moments later, my canvas bag appeared at the top of the ladder at the end of a bracelet-cluttered wrist. I hooked the strap with my foot and dragged the bag close enough to open it. I pulled a handful of white sage leaves out of a plastic bag and tossed them towards the stinky part of the attic, then threw on a few handfuls of charcoal granules for good measure and scooted towards the attic ladder.

The sage is a traditional purification herb. I'd normally recommend burning it, but that can freak out the normals.

The charcoal is just to absorb odors. That section of the attic reeks.

I stepped onto the hallway carpet and unfolded myself into a standing position. Shaking some insulation out of the left leg of my jeans onto the clean carpet was petty, if cathartic.

I walked into the affected bedroom and gestured towards the sheetrock over the window, the other side of what I'd found in the attic.

Addressing the teenage occupant of the room, I said, "I dropped some herbs up there, but that won't be the end of it."

The girl's mother stood in the doorway. She had originally contacted me about the situation, so I gave her the standard speech:

"You've got a visitor. Don't talk to it. Don't acknowledge it.

For the love of God, don't tell it that it's welcome to stay."

"That ghost hunter show said we should be respectful," she started.

"This is your house," I explained, suppressing a sigh. "You have a guest who has overstayed its welcome. Don't be rude, but you didn't invite it to visit, and it is vital you don't give it any ideas about staying."

"Who is... was... who was it?" Asked the girl.

"I don't know, and it doesn't matter."

But I did know, and it could.

Real estate disclosure laws in Georgia don't require notification that a death occurred in the home or if a former resident died in the house or somewhere else after moving out. This is a new house anyway, so this haunting isn't tied to the actual structure.

I do know that the area where it was built was formerly a forest where a bunch of children's bodies were recovered in the late seventies. They convicted a man for the murders, but that doesn't automatically put a spirit to rest.

This isn't what I'd consider a true spirit anyway. It's an echo.

When a place is the site of a strong emotion—fear, rage, or even love—that emotional energy doesn't always dissipate. The events that took place in that location repeat, over and over in a loop.

It can happen without anyone dying, and that makes research kind of a bitch.

In this case, the spirit itself has moved on to wherever it is spirits go after death, but an emotional remnant was still manifesting itself. The family has heard footsteps in the attic where there isn't even room to comfortably crawl.

That doesn't mean there's no danger. It's like buying a baby alligator before scoping out a sewer opening to dump it in when you've fed it enough for it to be large and dangerous.

You feed a haunting attention, and it isn't too long before you've got a beast too big to safely house near people.

On the other hand, if you leave it alone long enough, the energy will dissipate on its own.

Ignoring the emotions of the living isn't as easy, but I wish it was. It's my go-to move.

"Pretend it isn't there, and eventually it won't be," I said, moving my tools from my pockets into my messenger bag.

"Fake it until you make it?" The girl asked.

"I prefer 'feed a ghoul and starve a revenant,' but whatever works for you."

"So, it isn't a threat?" The girl couldn't move without rattling bracelets at me like some shaman. Hot Topic must make serious bank off the haunted.

"Avoid the attic for now. Store your Christmas decorations in the garage. The sounds you are hearing are disturbing, I'm sure, but harmless." I was pinned between the gazes of the teen and her mother like some rainforest beetle on a corkboard.

I swung the bag over my shoulder and moved towards the front door. "If things get worse or weird, you've got my number."

"You'll come back?" The mother tried to use an authoritative tone that probably didn't ever work on her daughter. It doesn't even slow me down.

"Absolutely," I painted on what I wanted to be a reassuring smile. "Worse and weird is what I do best."

I wadded my messenger bag into the suitcase in the trunk of my rental car. Carrying an EMF detector, flashing remote sensors, and several pounds of nine-volt batteries through the TSA checkpoint is a mistake a person only makes once. I was already uncomfortably close to missing my flight home.

Too much time later, I'd wedged myself into a business-class seat and entered the case notes for the Atlanta attic crawl. I mean, I also updated my actual work notes from the rest of the Atlanta trip, but those notes are less interesting.

For the record, I'd been on the clock reworking the

privileged access policies for a publicly traded company with a data center in Atlanta, but I try to use my frequent work travel to schedule paranormal excursions.

Online, I have two lives.

My professional profile is all computer security and sober photos of me at my friend's weddings.

My actual profile, with a carefully selected fake name, gets into the ghost stuff. I consult with varied paranormal teams, mostly here in the US, about their weirder cases.

I write articles about the paranormal and participate in research efforts. I spend an uncomfortable amount of time on paranormal message boards and "Creepy Twitter."

I don't take every case. Here's a secret: Sometimes people contact me after seeing some ghost hunt TV show, and my rigorously trained internal "crazy pants" detector flashes the red LEDs at me. In those instances, I jot down their address and promise to cross-check against a map of Native American burial grounds.

There is no such map.

We basically built this whole country on Native American burial grounds. That probably explains a lot about America.

When a family is struggling with an issue with the unknown, I try to help. Especially if there are children involved. In my experience, kids suffer the most because adults have had years to develop their personal filters. We adults can compartmentalize, and what we know shouldn't be real, we can disbelieve. Or we can drink it away.

Kids need someone to believe them. Sometimes, the monster in the closet is actually a monster, and sometimes, the best thing you can do for someone who is scared is to listen to them.

My professional life is built around best practices and repeatable results, but I try to apply the same standards to my ghost hunting.

Sometimes, ghosts just make some tapping noises or muffled voices, and those can be (and usually are) the changing acoustics in aging houses. Sometimes, it is both, but the mostly quiet, seldom active entities are rarely dangerous enough to worry about. If some phenomenon can be explained as anything other than haunting, I categorize it as that thing and move on.

Rarely, a haunting will be more blatant. Apparitions, moving objects, electrical fires with no discernible cause, and ghosts causing physical or emotional harm are harder to write off as a house settling. Those cases take more work, but reducing the risks to the living residents makes it worth it.

Once I get back home to Houston, I've got three days to catch up on paperwork and do laundry and do some research into a possible paranormal event at the Fountain House hotel in Austin.

Chapter Two

This would be far from my first haunted Texas hotel. It's almost a theme around here. I don't get invited to investigate them often, but a little light research can turn up some interesting stories, and a person can typically book a haunted room with a simple conversation with whoever is running the front desk.

When you want to do this, I advise that you don't ask if the hotel is haunted if you know that it is already from your own research. Do not go into this discussion with that level of gentleness. You're likely to get a denial because no one naturally wants to admit that they believe in ghosts. Only crazy people admit to seeing ghosts. You've got to go first.

"So," you'd casually ask, "how haunted is this place?"

You've admitted to your own belief in the supernatural or at least outed yourself as ghost-curious. I have never, not once, not gotten a story about a haunting after admitting that first.

In September of 1900, a Category Four hurricane hit the island city of Galveston, Texas, gutting St. Mary's Orphan Asylum. The resident nuns had tethered themselves to their ninety-three young charges with a clothesline in an attempt to stay together as the storm surged around them, wind and rain whipping the island with a viciousness that would devastate even modern buildings.

There were three survivors from the orphanage found clinging to a tree in the days after the storm had passed, their doomed companions scattered across the island, some still wrapped in the ultimately ineffective cord. The hurricane of 1900 killed at least six thousand people and possibly twice that, so recovery was a hurried and incomplete process. The bodies of the nuns and orphans were most often buried where they were found, scattered for miles inland along the path of the storm.

In 1911, the luxurious Hotel Galvez was built along the beach, almost certainly on top of a number of these hastily dug, unmarked graves. It was a destination for the wealthy, a popular wedding and event venue like the Fountain House in Austin, bedecked in palm trees, ornate columns, and gilded furniture.

An even larger storm hit the island in 1915, and the Hotel Galvez hosted the first recorded hurricane party. Sure, almost three hundred people were killed in the freshly rebuilt city, but the champagne never stopped flowing at the Hotel Galvez.

The dark wooden bar top in the lobby was salvaged from the Old Galveston Club, which was a secret speakeasy back in the days of Prohibition. Legend says that the margarita was invented on that bar top in the 1940s, while the Hotel Galvez served as office space and housing for the Coast Guard during the Second World War. The bar top took its home at the Hotel Galvez about fifty years later.

Presidents slept there. The fanciest families married their kids to each other there. The richest elbows in the state rubbed each other and then got exfoliated in the spa on location.

And the fifth floor is haunted all to hell.

I stayed on the fifth floor one Halloween. I don't know about that "thinning of the veil between the living and the dead" stuff, but I heard plenty of voices, and my equipment burned through batteries as it recorded activity all up and down the hall.

When I finally went to sleep, I was awakened several times by a presence in the room and I could see a dark figure in the bathroom reflected in the long mirror next to the door.

I never got up to investigate. If someone wants to watch me sleep from the bathroom, learning anything about their motivations isn't likely to make me feel any better.

Chapter Three

While documenting the process for requesting a firewall exception is, without a doubt, compelling reading, I will just say that it went "okay."

I'd gotten home and tended to the cat litter and verified the food situation for Aengus. It's not that the cat sitter had done a poor job. She actually had probably left my apartment less than an hour before I'd arrived.

That's not the point. The point is that I have responsibilities, and Aengus, an elderly Burmese I picked up at the shelter because he bit me and I'm a sucker, expects me to hold those up.

According to fossil records, more than 30,000 years ago, humans began an association with a particular species of wolf. They were the apex predator in much of the human range, and these canines gladly traded that status for access to food and belly rubs in exchange for serving as protection for us humans with our blunt teeth, stubby claws, and infinitely chewable flesh. And they eventually became dogs in their adorable infinite variety.

In the paranormal community, it is generally accepted that this protective instinct developed into an awareness that exceeds our own. Dogs can just see things in the spiritual realm that you and I are just blind to.

I love dogs.

On the other hand, about 11,000 years ago, newly agrarian humans started producing enough grain to have a need to store it. This drew in birds and rodents to steal this grain. And the birds and rodents drew in cats.

The cats decided to stay for the birds and rodents, which was their entire purpose, but at some point, there was a negotiation where they would also get canned food and unlimited affection (but only on their terms, communicated by violence). Cats never evolved that protective, vigilant trait. They don't see ghosts any better than your average person. And unless that ghost is actively trying to steal from your winter grain supplies, there is almost no chance your cat is going to be bothered by it.

Aengus tolerates me because I'm warm when I sleep. Neither of us has any illusions about that. I respect it.

And I don't want him to see anything horrifying that I'm oblivious to.

The Fountain House in Austin was entirely too interesting to leave unresearched.

First built in 1885, the ownership of the hotel really got interesting in the 1980s. A slew of bankruptcies saw the hotel change hands a number of times. It's a huge building—half a city block, with a few hundred rooms and a massive waiting list for the ballrooms for fancy weddings.

The building has collected ghost stories in sedimentary layers over the decades it has been in operation.

The current owners, Fountain House Holdings LLC, have requested a "quiet" consultation regarding one of the more famous haunted rooms.

Room 318 is notorious. Two brides have died there just before their own scheduled fancy weddings, and now the room is customarily left unoccupied. At least, that was the custom before Fountain House Holdings LLC.

Fountain House Holdings LLC would like to make the room available to "paranormal enthusiasts" for ghost-themed events, and, more importantly, they'd like a "professional" to certify the room as safe.

It may come as a surprise, but there is no certification that makes a location actually safe when it comes to hauntings.

But if someone has access to a location where multiple people have seen an entity with no easy explanation, I'm all about it. The opportunity to set up equipment in Room 318 and to also ghost-hunt a whole reportedly haunted building is my kryptonite, that is, if a fictional mineral could technically modify the current state of our ability to interact with the dead.

Even without the ghost bride stories, there are many documented deaths on-site. So many that it is tempting to say that not finding evidence would be the strangest result.

My company had set me up in a decent enough hotel in Austin's tech corridor, but I was really planning to camp out in Room 316 at the Fountain House Hotel.

"Reservation for Lawrence Miller," I told the desk clerk.

He performed the slowest slow blink I'd ever personally witnessed before putting an insincere smile on his face.

"Mister Miller, we've been expecting you."

"Thank you, Thad," I answered, having read his name tag. "I won't be any trouble."

"Of course not," he waved his hands quite unconvincingly. "Let me get the owners down to show you what they want."

After a few whispered phone calls, I was assured I'd be given a full tour as soon as possible. I handed my baggage off to a bellhop and headed for the bar to wait.

Ms. Anderson of Fountain House LLC left me waiting for exactly 60% of an Old Fashioned. I've waited for less attractive company through worse drinks, so this wasn't an immediate red flag.

Gloria Anderson was at least ten years too young to be a real estate magnate. Her blonde hair was tightly product-ed into place, and her blazer and skirt proclaimed her familiarity with the Ann Taylor outlet in Corsicana an hour south.

I smiled and extended my hand. "I'm Lawrence Miller. I'm excited to have the opportunity to investigate this property."

"Aren't the stories just fantastic?" She glowed. "We have a waiting list of paranormal groups who want exactly this experience, and your review can only improve that."

"I suppose it can if I find anything," I offered. "Have you experienced anything paranormal yourself?"

"Personally? No. But we have several long-term staff members who swear the third floor is cursed."

"And you believe them?" I asked.

"We believe the history of the hotel lends itself to a unique clientele and hope to provide them with a premium experience."

Ah.

"If it is 'cursed,' do you have any interest in fixing it?"

Gloria sipped at a glass of white wine. "Not especially."

"Good," I tipped my own glass up to finish my drink. "Because I don't do that. I can tell you if I find evidence of a haunting, but I won't pretend I can stop it."

"Perfect," she agreed. "No one cares to rent a room that used to be haunted."

An hour later, I'd wired 318 with EMF detectors, IR cameras, and night vision.

It was clear on the walk-through that 318 had long been out of use for guests. The fixtures were dusty, and the wallpaper was in a style I'd call "vintage" if I were trying to sell it. It boasted two full-size beds and a medium-sized television with an actual tube-type screen. It did not turn on, and the clock radio alarm on the nightstand also refused to light up. They may have just died of natural causes. Both dated to the 1970s, but active hauntings are hard on even modern electrical appliances.

I set a digital voice recorder next to the clock radio and left the room.

I don't pretend to be sensitive to spiritual activity. I would say, and most of my managers in tech would agree, reading a room is not in my skill set. That said, room 318 (in addition to threatening my dust allergy) was pretty creepy in the way places are when the living don't visit them often.

I set up two monitors and a laptop in room 316, half-watched, and half-worked on a checklist for my project in the morning. The tech company that had hired me was having issues with change management. It's not unique to Texas to have technicians make cowboy changes, but that doesn't make the shareholders any happier.

As the shadows of the much taller buildings surrounding the Fountain Hotel cast the building into early twilight, room 318 started to live up to the expectations.

I started to see the EMF detectors flash blue as the sunlight gradually died. The simple devices won't record, but they light up fine for the video recording and can indicate where to look when I review the footage later.

I glanced back at the monitor as the LED on the nightstand flashed, and the infrared camera registered movement. The voice recorder had fallen off the nightstand.

I hit the hallway running and burst into 318 with a flashlight and EMF detector, ready to face the weird and worse.

That's not what I found at all.

Having specifically set the voice recorder in the middle of the nightstand and further having been monitoring the room through multiple cameras, I knew no one had been in the room to push the recorder off the table. Being able to eliminate a human source for an event is still a long way from confirming a paranormal cause.

The battery on the voice recorder was completely dead.

Dead batteries are to be expected when you leave a camera or recorder running nonstop for hours, but sudden drains can indicate that something is leeching energy from the area. For what? Possibly manifestation, but also possibly you got a bad batch of batteries, so who really knows?

Damn my adherence to the scientific method. I could have a cushy gig on the Travel Channel if I was just willing to fling assumptions at the restless dead like my peers.

The sound of breaking glass in the bathroom interrupted my hate fest.

I ran to the hotel bathroom, flipped on the light, and looked around. The mirror was intact. Both glasses were still wrapped in plastic bags and sitting in the plastic tray.

I saw no shards of glass anywhere.

I turned back to the main room, and the heavy glass ashtray from the nightstand hit me right between the eyes.

Consciousness decided I should be abandoned like a bad investment, and everything went black.

Chapter Four

Dawn is a bitch. Especially if it's only showing up to highlight your bad decisions.

A touch to my forehead let me know I was nursing a bruise I'd need to cover with makeup or a good story.

The heavy ashtray was back on the nightstand.

I groaned and sat up.

I had been sprawled out in front of the door like I'd been shot from the hallway. Exactly like the woman who had been shot by her paramour in the 1930s.

Again, there's no way to certify a haunting, but holy crap, sometimes you just want a warning sign or something.

You want to know the surest remedy for the morning after you've experienced some paranormal nonsense?

Brunch.

I hit the hotel restaurant with a visible facial bruise. I could've hit up a Walgreens, but, in my experience, waffles take precedence. Instead, I hit the omelette bar. Three eggs, Swiss cheese, mushrooms, and green onions.

I took a quick shower and hurriedly dressed in black jeans, a dress shirt rakishly skipping the collar button, and a tie only loosely holding up the illusion of a dress code.

Black cowboy boots I'd bought in a moment of weakness and a tweed sport coat with suede patches on the elbows completed the look as I grabbed my laptop bag and headed to get my rental car out of valet parking.

Ghosts expect people to notice the ways they influence their environment, and IT consultants work under the same conditions. In both cases, costuming is 80% of the job.

I exchanged a couple of text messages with Ms. Anderson during the day and agreed to meet with her for an update at 9pm at the Blind Pig Pub, about a block away from the hotel.

The drinks are a little cheaper than at the hotel bar, but more importantly, there's a large courtyard open to the sky where I could sit under a tree and ground myself in preparation for another overnight with the restless dead in 318.

Gloria Anderson was there when I arrived a few minutes early. I paused at the table she had claimed to wave and then walked to the bar to pick up a drink before returning and sitting across from her, the string of lights finally illuminating my face.

"What happened to you?" she seemed genuinely confused.

"A vintage ashtray in your non-smoking hotel pitched itself across the room, and I wasn't wearing a catcher's mask." I had told an entirely different story to my tech client about a low-speed collision on I-35 that triggered the airbag and smacked me in the face with the Honda emblem from the steering wheel of my rental car.

"So, I guess you've established the room is haunted and not safe?"

"It's definitely not safe if you're not wearing some kind of sports equipment, but I've got a few days more here, and I'd like to continue to investigate. I got hit in the doorway to the bathroom and woke up in front of the front door. There's something going on there that is going to continue to send messages, and if they insist on being violent, it isn't the best case for amateur ghost hunters."

I really didn't want her to cut off my access, but more than that, I didn't want her charging a premium to send people into a situation where they would be hurt.

"Go back tonight if you want. Validate the activity, and your sign-off is all we need." She took a leisurely sip of something frozen. "First impressions, do you think it's one of the legendary brides?"

"It's something angry. Dying before your wedding could certainly generate the type of emotions that would result in violent activity."

We chatted a bit more and finished our drinks. People in

Texas can share a lot of words around our opinions on tacos and the places that sell them.

I waited for her car to arrive before I walked back to my room to review the footage from the night before.

What they don't really highlight on those ghost-hunting TV shows is the hours and hours of reviewing video files where nothing happens.

The camera on the nightstand did capture me getting hit in the face, which set my forehead to throbbing again, though the embarrassment was arguably more painful. Seeing yourself bonelessly crumple to the floor is just unflattering.

The camera angles didn't capture my migration to the front door or the return of the ashtray to the nightstand.

All I had for a night's work was some sound files, a head wound, and more questions.

The footage from the day ended at about 2 pm as the batteries died.

I walked over to 318 to swap them out and reset everything for another night.

The room was cold. So cold that it felt damp. The air conditioner under the window wasn't running. I wasn't even sure it still worked.

The smell was new. Mildewed rose petals and dusty linen. I did a quick sweep with my EMF detector and, finding nothing, returned to my room next door. I stared at the monitors for a few minutes and verified the video was recording.

Nothing was moving. The temperature was stable. I tapped a screen in case that was suddenly the fix for frozen video.

Feeling restless, I grabbed a few things and took the stairs down to the hotel bar to pass some time. An Irish coffee slowly vanished in front of me over the next hour. I told myself I needed the caffeine.

I knew the ghost stories before taking the case, but (as much as I love ghost stories), they typically take on elements of folklore over time. The facts become muddled by history and the simple passage of time. I pulled up old newspaper articles.

I found records of both brides. In 1895, Judith Mounier's death the day before her wedding was ruled a suicide, and in 1932, Anne-Marie Bertrand had been shot by her fiancé. It didn't state a motive, but there was an unnamed man listed as a witness.

Neither report listed a room number, but I couldn't rule out 318.

Stewart Simms tried to rob the bank across the street in 1929 and ran from the police into the hotel lobby, where he was shot and killed by a guest of the hotel. Texas, right?

In 1972, a groundskeeper was electrocuted trying to repair the courtyard fountain.

When you add in long-term staff, who could develop an attachment to the property no matter where they technically died, and the fact that almost 100,000 people die in hotels every year, the list of possible ghosts gets very long very quickly.

I couldn't find anything conclusive about the reported sound of children running on the third floor, but plenty of kids stay in hotels. I think I had seen a couple of living ones that afternoon.

As I finished the last (now cold) sip a woman sat down across from me at the tiny corner table I'd staked out. She took in the stacks of paper to my left and right and the widescreen laptop in front of me and squeezed a stemmed glass full of a dark liquid onto the narrow band of table I had neglected to clutter behind my screen.

She was pretty, bookish, and very pale, especially given her ink-black hair. She wore a chunky sweater over a flowing short dress. There was a sizable crystal wrapped in silver wire on a chain around her neck. Well-worn combat boots were tucked under the table, crossed at the ankles.

"You're the ghost hunter," she said by way of greeting.

Invading my clearly claimed space wasn't enough, apparently. She needed to start with an accusation.

I mean, sure, she was right, but a greeting still might have been nice.

"Sometimes I am. I'm Lawrence Miller."

"No," she shook her head, "You're really not."

I went for my driver's license, and she gestured for me to stop, "You're not a Larry, either."

"Larry Miller is an actor," I explained.

"Pretty Woman?"

"Necessary Roughness," I corrected.

"L.A. Story," she offered.

"10 Things I Hate About You," I said with finality.

She looked me up and down before nodding once sharply and announcing, "You are a Lair."

Great. I'd been reduced to a diminutive.

"Gloria said I'd probably find you here. She sent me to help." She smiled at me.

I didn't smile back.

"Why? She didn't mention you earlier this evening, and I

have a process I don't feel like explaining, Miss . . ."

"Meghan O'Leary," she offered her hand, which I shook out of reflex. "I have my own process, and it won't interfere with yours. Gloria said that given the obvious danger", she gestured at my head, "you could use some backup, Lair."

"I've never needed it before, and I'm comfortable with that. I've got electronic eyes on the room right now, and I'm logging temperature variations. I'll go back in there in a bit and guard my soft bits. How can you help?"

She smiled again, and I found it unsettling, but I tend to feel that way about smiles.

"I'm a psychic and an emotional empath."

I may have been boiled down, distilled into a Lair, but I wouldn't order new business cards just yet.

I love words. They are the bedrock of my existence, and I use them to frame my entire world.

"Well," I pronounced with both dignity and eloquence, "fuck."

Chapter Five

One time, years ago, I spent a weekend at the Menger Hotel in San Antonio.

If you're looking for a location that is likely haunted, you'd have to hit up an Airbnb at Gettysburg to compete.

And absolutely, if you've got a vacation rental at Gettysburg, you should go to that. Why is that even a discussion?

Anyway, The Menger Hotel in San Antonio has every reason to be haunted.

It is built on the grounds of (and is still across the street from) the Alamo, which Texans are required by law to remember. I had Texas History twice (fourth and seventh grade) in Texas Public School, and while I have recovered well, I can't pretend there isn't a reverent reflex.

German immigrants William and Mary Menger opened the hotel in 1859, right in the plaza with the revered Alamo Mission. They put it up with money from the Menger Brewery, the first place in Texas to brew beer and the largest brewery in the state for decades. William Menger bought up competing breweries for years, eventually earning the nickname "the beer king" in the area and cementing the influence of German immigrants in the Texas hill country forever.

The Menger Hotel was the fanciest hotel on the continent as far west as it was for an obscenely long time.

Like the Fountain House, it cycled through owners and refurbishments as the standards of "fancy" changed over the decades.

What didn't change was the downstairs Menger Bar, old oak, crystal, and ample mirrors, all supplied by an earlier, post-prohibition designer.

The Menger Bar, which looks out over a side street, across the carefully tended cactus gardens, and into the south wall of the Alamo, was a hangout for Teddy Roosevelt. He used it as a place to recruit his famous Rough Riders for the Spanish-American War.

Across from the bar top itself is a raised area a few steps up, which is perpetually a bit darker, dimmer than it should be even when it is bright daylight outside. The area is quiet, with the typical bar sounds muted by some odd effect of the wood surrounding everything.

The beer is cold, and the crowd is perpetually refreshed with hotel guests and tourists. But you can really imagine, sitting there, surrounded by the uniforms of the 1st United States Volunteer Cavalry, cowboys from New Mexico, Oklahoma, and Texas arriving to speak with Roosevelt and sign up to fight for Cuban independence. As someone who buys their Cuban rum at Duty-Free,

I honestly and wholeheartedly endorse this whole process.

The weekend I stayed there I spent a healthy amount of time in the bar but more time in the elegantly appointed hotel room.

I heard voices that weren't recorded and recorded voices I didn't hear. I saw shadows in hallways and apparitions in conference rooms.

Items rearranged themselves in my room, and a full glass of whiskey launched itself across that haunted bar to shatter against the door to the street. The bartender didn't bat an eye as she replaced my drink.

This was an accepted event. Just the cost of doing business in a haunted hotel.

I woke up on Saturday night with something shaking my bed like a rugby team bouncing on the memory foam with the metallic rattle of spurs around my head. I had no idea how to catalogue and quantify that experience.

Maybe Gettysburg is nice.

It probably depends on the time of year.

Chapter Six

Meghan didn't have a key to 318, so we stopped by my room to pick up some gear and drop off my laptop. She took in my tiny working area lit only by the glow of the monitors and the associated tangle of assorted charging cables. She noticed the equipment bag and the much smaller sprawl of my garment bag.

She saw the rocks glass on the nightstand next to the half-empty bottle of Powers whiskey but didn't comment.

I unlocked room 318 and stepped inside to check the equipment.

Meghan stood in the doorway, her eyes closed and her fingertips lightly resting on the door frame.

The batteries were all fine, and the cameras were still all facing where I'd pointed them. The room was as cold as it had been before, but layered over the dried rose and linen smell was a heady musk of some kind - masculine and less than clean. I ducked my head down to make sure I hadn't somehow made the most severe hygiene error of my life.

It wasn't me.

"It's not you," Meghan said from the doorway.

I looked over and her eyes were still closed.

"Of course, it isn't me," I replied, "Don't be ridiculous."

She smiled again without opening her eyes. "Of course."

I was pretty sure I hated her.

"Sadness and anger in here," her forehead wrinkled slightly, "It's like they are struggling over which is dominant."

"Emotions are struggling, or entities are struggling?" It would be nice to know the motivation the next time an ashtray took flight.

The light dimmed like a cloud passing over the sun - except that the blinds were closed, and it was dark outside. The thermometers both beeped to mark a drop in temperature, and I saw my breath fog when I exhaled.

"Definitely angry," Meghan stepped into the room, eyes open finally.

I glanced unconsciously at the nightstand and the potential glass projectile on top. It hadn't moved, but it looked like moisture was beading on the surface.

Meghan pointed towards the far corner of the room and said, "It's here now."

I saw the curtain move slightly before I noticed the dark shadow next to it.

It was easily seven feet tall, pitch black at what would be center mass on a living person, and less distinct towards the edges.

It loomed.

My handheld EMF detector was pegged in the red for a few seconds before going dark.

I looked around and saw that the red LEDs on the cameras were all dark as well.

Turning back, I couldn't tell if the entity was darker or more solid or if the room itself had dimmed further.

It drifted forward, and I stepped between it and Meghan.

"Step back outside. I'll follow you," I said over my shoulder, never taking my eyes off the dark form.

I couldn't see through the shape at all now, and I could make out the outlines of legs and arms, which were longer than the arms of a proportionate human.

I backed towards the door, my shuffling steps seeming obscenely loud in the unnatural silence that clotted the room.

Then I heard the breathing. It seemed to come from all directions at once, wet, hissing gasps like someone drowning but loudly.

Looking back, I saw the shadow had moved closer to me. It

started to slowly raise its right arm in my direction when I decided I needed to be moving more quickly.

I turned back towards the door, took a step with my right foot, and then pitched forward when my left foot was tangled in something - the phone cord. I heard a jingling crash to my left as the old Bakelite phone was pulled off the nightstand and onto the carpet.

The floor had been clear of obstructions every time I'd checked it, including when I'd just walked across it a few moments before.

I flipped over onto my back and sat up, moving to disentangle my left foot. The shadow seemed to lunge into me, and a shocking cold filled me, locking my joints into place and making my heart shudder. I couldn't see out. I couldn't see anything. It felt like my nose, mouth, throat, and lungs were filled with ice-cold bog water.

I couldn't breathe.

A voice whispered through the room. Or through my head. It was difficult to tell.

"What have you done?" it choked out around watery gasps. "What have you done to me?"

Pressure seemed to build up in my skull while the cold

soaked into my bones. I couldn't move my chest enough to take a decent breath, but it didn't feel like oxygen deprivation, exactly. It felt like a direct pressure. A cold weight centered in the middle of my brain like a frost burned brick.

I decided it couldn't hurt to just lie down. I could take a quick nap and wake up later with a fresh, rested approach to this problem. And it was already dark enough that going to sleep would just be easy.

It made perfect sense. Why would I fight that?

Sometimes, there's absolutely nothing that can be heard over the call of nonexistence.

"Get out!" Meghan yelled behind me.

And I tried. Really, I did. I mumbled as much as the light returned, and I could move again.

"I wasn't talking to you," she knelt and helped me get the phone cord off.

I stood and kicked the cord back under the bed and out of the way.

I considered grabbing the cameras to refresh the batteries, but Meghan shook her head.

"It's done for tonight." She seemed certain. "There's a fireplace in the lobby. You should sit near it for a bit."

I didn't argue with her.

Chapter Seven

I know that hot chocolate and peppermint schnapps is technically called a peppermint patty, but I had the dignity to decline the mini marshmallows.

Mesquite wood popped as it burned hot in the oversized stone fireplace, and I sat as close as I comfortably could. The chill was no longer debilitating, but it hadn't completely fled my joints. Or my head.

In addition to the knot on my forehead, I now had a twinge in my left knee and what I suspected would be a glorious bruise on my right side from the fall, as well as carpet burns on both arms up to the elbows.

I tried to concentrate on the cocoa. It wasn't that great.

My clinical approach to a haunting had failed me. If I had been alone, I might have died. Or worse.

My body was increasingly battered, and the part of a ghost hunt I was good at was long over.

Meghan sat across from me, politely quiet, as if she was respectful of the time I needed.

She had opted for the marshmallows, and I'll admit now that they seemed like a good call.

I knew she was waiting for me to ask. To admit I didn't have all the answers. To legitimize her calling and acknowledge that I was in over my head.

"So, this is powdered hot chocolate mix, isn't it?" I really tried.

She stared into the fire for a moment and didn't ask. "That wasn't the first time you were attacked."

Finding the burning wood equally enchanting, I admitted, "No. But it doesn't exactly happen every week, either. And it has never happened like that on an investigation."

"That wasn't the only entity in room 318," she offered.

"So, was it sadness, or was it anger?" I didn't know why I felt that information might help.

She thought for a second. "It was anger at first and sadness at the end. You heard the questions, right? I know you did."

"Yeah, what did I do?" The one thing I was certain of was that I personally hadn't done anything to the occupants of room 318.

"It seems like the entity thought I was someone else. Could this be a residual? Like it just does that at 11:06 PM on certain days or moon phases or when Mercury is in Gatorade or something?"

"Don't roll your eyes," she admonished, "you have a head wound."

I held up a hand in surrender, "No offense. That's not the side of the street I normally work on."

"It's not an echo. It attacked you on purpose." She seemed certain. "Now, from that brief interaction, I couldn't say for sure whether it was intended to hurt you or just a poor attempt at communication."

"I'm not in a hurry to get us a larger sample size," I wrapped both hands around my hot chocolate after waving at the bartender for another round.

"No kidding," she said," How is the leg?"

"My head is worse," I produced a sheet of rough notes from my jacket pocket. "I've got at least a partial list of suspects. Look it over and see if anything clicks?"

Judith Mounier.

Stewart Simms.

Anne-Marie Bertrand.

Michael Gonzales.

None of them listed dates or cause of death. Just names.

She looked over the list for a while. Our fresh drinks arrived. Both had marshmallows. Fine. Damn it.

"Anne-Marie," she stared off into the middle distance.

"Anne-Marie is angry. How did she die?"

"Her fiancé shot her for adultery," I poured the leftover cocoa from the first drink into the second in an attempt to cool it enough to make it drinkable immediately.

"There's more to that story." She hadn't stopped staring. I uncomfortably looked over my own shoulder to make sure I wasn't missing something back there.

"Not in the papers," I know I'd gone through every article and had copies in my room. "More as in another victim or some other motive? There was a witness, a man, but he wasn't named by the journalist."

"Why not? Was it too scandalous for a reporter to spill?"

I hadn't considered why. I'd gotten too used to working with incomplete information.

"It was fairly scandalous with the boyfriend and the murder and everything," I didn't know enough about the motivations of 1930s Texas newspapermen.

"That's not it," she shook her head and blinked at me. "Can you meet me tomorrow at around noon a few blocks from here? I've got a friend who can help."

"I'm already uncomfortable as Batman and Robin," I met her eyes, "I don't want to form the Super Friends."

"Don't worry! You'll love him!" She fired off a text message and got a response almost immediately, which is impressive (or concerning) for after midnight. "He works your side of the street."

"Fine," I finished my drink and paid the tab. "I guess we need all the information we can get."

"Damn right we do," she handed me a business card with an address on Guadeloupe Street and turned to exit the lobby, "See you at noon, Robin."

I was pretty sure I still hated her. But maybe a little bit less.

I'm on a quiet cul-de-sac, looking at the front of a comfortably worn house. Walking up the front steps, I can't help but look up at the beadboard ceiling over the small front porch. It's covered in spiderwebs and abandoned wasp nests.

It's light blue. Powdery blue. Like the memory of a robin's egg.

I go inside and bear right for the dining room and liquor cabinet. I pour a generous cup of whiskey and wave away the cackling mob of things in the kitchen to get to the deck over the backyard.

I lean on the railing and light a cigarette, holding it and the drink like crucifixes against an intangible darkness.

The dead children play in the backyard between the pine trees and the withering rose bush hedges. I can't hear them, but I can see them talking.

They clasp their hands and circle, ringing around the rosy across the lawn. Across the pool. Across more of the lawn. Around the corner of the house.

"Oh, fuck this," I take another drink. I don't go back inside right away. I don't remember going back inside at all.

Chapter Eight

I texted Gloria in the morning on the way to my day job and let her know I'd been attacked and that there was more research to be done. I didn't detail my injuries out of concern she would pull us off the case entirely for insurance reasons.

I blocked out my work calendar for a couple of hours around lunch.

The Austin Historical Center is, as one would expect, in an older building in the historic district.

I parked my rental car in an open space out front and waited.

Meghan pulled into the spot next to mine in a Japanese subcompact a few minutes later. She waved.

I climbed out of the car and waved back before walking towards the wraparound porch of the Historical Center.

The door was locked.

"Beau will be here shortly," Meghan told me.

"Beau?"

"Beau Neumann. He's the archivist here."

I looked back at the door.

"Part-time?" I tried again. Yeah, it was still locked.

"They aren't open all the time. It's basically by appointment only," she explained.

"Meghan, darling!" A man shouted from the sidewalk, hustling up and jingling an enormous ring of keys in one hand.

He seemed to shake with excitement, a five-foot-six balding little man in a peach sweater vest and linen slacks.

"How are you, Beau?" Meghan beamed at him, nudging me with an elbow.

"Mr. Neumann! I'm Lawrence Miller! It's nice to meet you, having heard so many nice things," I lied.

"Nonsense! You ghost hunters appreciate history in a way few others do! The pleasure is mine!" He seemed sincere. I worried about his mental health.

He unlocked the door and gestured grandly for us to proceed with him inside.

The entryway was all dark wood and Native American art. There was an oil painting of a cowboy next to a campfire in front of what looked like a modern version of tribal pottery. I wanted to check for a Made in China tag on the bottom, but I was almost certain it had actually been produced on one of the reservations.

Beau hadn't stopped talking. I'm pretty sure he hadn't even slowed down since the sidewalk.

"Oh, you know me, Meghan!" He ushered us into what I guessed was his office. "I'm running all over town to settle last-minute details for the fundraiser this weekend, and one of the interns decided we needed a new filing system, which she implemented all on her own, and now we can't find anything!"

He sat in a cowhide desk chair and gestured to two non-wheeled ones across a leather-topped desk that would probably qualify as a county in any state but Texas.

There were actual longhorns on the front, truly the Texas Cadillac of office furniture.

"We won't take too much of your time," Meghan assured him, "We just need to know why some information might have been left out of an old newspaper article. And if you can fill in the blanks, that would be even better."

"Nonsense, Meghan," he practically beamed, "I know all the living gossip already. Our chats are the only way I can know what the dead are up to."

"This is about a murder in a hotel downtown in 1932," I started.

"Anne-Marie!" He finished for me, "Oh, I know Anne-Marie!"

I was impressed. "Why wasn't her killer named? There

weren't even any engagement records on file, and there was a witness to the crime who also seemed to be a mystery."

"That's because even the state capital can be a small town in some ways," he smiled a little pensively, "everyone who needed to know already knew the fiancé, and it wasn't the business of anyone else in 1932."

"Who was he?" Meghan asked.

"Robert 'Bobby' Rose was his name," he looked at us from under an arched eyebrow.

"I'm drawing a blank, Beau," I tried to raise my own eyebrow but was harshly reminded of the bruise on my forehead. "But I'm from out of town."

"Let me guess! Houston!"

"What gave me away?" I asked.

"Composite soles on your boots. No reason to switch out the leather if you don't spend a lot of time walking on concrete."

If I had a cowboy hat, I'd have tipped it at him.

"Good catch," I nodded at him. "For a second, I thought you were another psychic."

He laughed a warm sound. It wasn't what I'd have expected from someone who called themselves an archivist.

"So, who was Bobby Rose?" I tried to steer the conversation back to the reason we were here.

"The Rose family owned one of the largest ranches in central Texas at the turn of the century." Beau leaned in conspiratorially. "They diversified from livestock in time to be major players in 'prohibition mitigation,'" he made with the air quotes. "By the time that was over, the Roses ran just about every kind of criminal enterprise in an area way larger than their original homestead. Prostitution, gambling, loan sharking, protection rackets. If there was money to be made, they made it. Bobby was the heir apparent."

"So obviously, his involvement would have been scrubbed from official records," Meghan supplied. "Powerful families and all that. What about the witness?"

"That's where we get into rumor territory," Beau smiled.

"Your favorite territory," she grinned back.

"The witness wasn't Anne-Marie's lover," Beau looked to the side as if to make sure no one was listening in this otherwise completely deserted building, "the consensus at the time was that he was an FBI man out of Dallas and Anne-Marie was turning state's evidence."

"Now we've got multiple possible motivations," I sighed. Why can't it ever be a simple desecrated Native American burial ground?

"Bobby was arrested immediately and charged with murder. Shooting a young woman in front of an officer of the law is tough for even the richest family to buy their way out of. He was killed in prison by a guard during an escape attempt." Beau shook his head, "the Rose family spent the next few decades under a federal magnifying glass. A lot of locals think Bobby's murder was paid for by the Roses in retaliation. The remaining Roses locally own a slaughterhouse which mostly supplies the local brisket scene. It's honest work, I'm sure, but it doesn't pay like crime either."

"Not really a very happy ending to the story," Meghan commented.

I know happy endings, and if there is such a thing, they don't result in the kind of hauntings I get called about.

"There is something of a symmetry here, though," Beau opened a massive ledger on his desk, found the section he was looking for, and traced down the columns on the left, "Birth records for the county, Anne-Marie Bertrand, born March 18, 1908."

I stared at him blankly.

"Anne-Marie came into the world on the date 3/18 and checked out of it from room 318," Meghan arrived at the destination ahead of me. I was becoming used to that, but that didn't mean I liked it.

"For anyone keeping score," I began to count off on fingers, "We've got murder, betrayal, incarceration, and mob hits."

"This is Austin, Mr. Miller," Beau grinned across the desk, "Someone is always keeping score."

Chapter Nine

I returned to work and hosted a meeting to explain the new secured process around accessing personal data about the company's user base. It was gripping.

But more importantly, the company had sprung for sandwiches, so I grabbed a couple because I'd skipped lunch.

My mind kept wandering back to room 318. What was supposed to have been a simple binary choice - Is the room haunted or not? - had transformed over a few encounters into a complicated and dangerous situation. I'd been injured, and I'd been prepared for a confrontation with the dead.

Signing off for others to unknowingly walk into that room was out of the question until we had mitigated some of that risk. If that actually meant untangling events almost a century old, I didn't know how to even begin.

In my usual ghost hunts, I identify the type of manifestation and advise the residents on how to interact with it or how not to, and then I ride off into the sunset. Ghostly motivations have never been a data point I especially cared about. Aren't the dead supposed to be beyond the reach of mortal concerns?

I met Meghan at the hotel bar after work, and we went over the game plan for the evening.

"No offense," she started, "but I don't think you lumbering around the room like an ox is our best move tonight."

"Offense taken," I objected, "I hardly think I 'lumber.'" I considered, "Maybe I'm a touch direct for our purposes."

"However you want to put it, you're a blunt object, and this poor woman was already murdered," she added, "and by a man, I must point out."

"Okay, so how do we approach tonight?"

Meghan offered, "I go in alone, first, and you watch on the monitor and be ready to pull me out."

I hadn't had a chance to review the footage from the last night when I'd been attacked. I would be watching it live tonight, I guess.

"That's not how I've ever done it," I started to object out of hand before realizing, "but then again, I've never had anyone to go in instead of me."

"We were both in there last night," she shuddered a bit, "and I knew there was trouble before you did. I felt it."

"Watch out for phone cords," I was just trying to be helpful while realizing there wasn't much else I could offer. "If you call out, I'll be right there. Don't take any unnecessary risks."

"I'll talk Anne-Marie down if I can," she seemed to be

assembling a plan as well as explaining it to me, "We know more than we did yesterday. I can try to put her to rest."

"You've had that work before?" I'd never seen it.

She nodded, "If I can correctly guess what's holding her here, I can help her to leave or convince her to not attack anyone else."

"I don't like it. How do we know she won't just wait for the next opportunity to reverse course and try to kill the first group of amateurs to rent out 318?"

"She's been angry for decades," she seemed certain, "it's like momentum. If I can redirect it, then at worst, it takes her decades to cut back towards violence."

"Really? Sounds like math," I wrinkled my forehead, and it hurt slightly less than the last time I tried that.

"Yeah," she patted down her pockets in a precise and practiced sequence, "the living are volatile. The dead have eternity to change their minds–if they ever do."

"Let's go." I stood up and headed for my room to feel useless, "Remember, I'm right next door and watching. Don't take chances and yell if things get weird."

The last thing I needed was a multi-angle view of someone getting hurt by a ghost 20 feet away from me while I sat in a desk chair.

I checked that all four video feeds were working and turned up the sound a bit. Too much and the feeds would overlap into a rapid WHUP-WHUP-WHUP sound that would increase in volume until I cranked it down or blew a speaker.

I drew the drapes closed to block any glare from my screen.

I nervously watched the screen as Meghan opened the door to 318 and stepped inside.

She quickly crossed to the window and slid open the vent on the air conditioner.

She took out a shiny metal tray and set it on the small desk across from the beds and placed a small bundle of something on it. She put something small in each corner of the room, and I was grateful when she started narrating.

"Lair, I just put smoky quartz chips in the corners to aid in manifestation. I'm going to salt the threshold of the main door to keep the spirits from crossing and then get started."

She produced a small plastic bag and laid out a line of powder across the front door.

"Now I'm going to light the sage, mugwort, and palo santo wood." She winked at one of the cameras, "all ethically sourced."

Smoke began to rise from the metal tray in thick, lazy

spirals.

Meghan climbed onto the bed and sat cross-legged. About 15 minutes went by while she seemed to do absolutely nothing else.

A beep to my left notified me that the temperature in 318 was dropping quickly. Shadows gathered near the ceiling, and my sound feeds began to pick up shuffling footsteps from multiple directions.

I tensed, leaning forward with my fingertips splayed at the edge of the desk.

I saw a rime of frost etch itself across the mirror before the lenses of the cameras started to fog over as well.

Suddenly, Meghan looked up at the door to the tiny bathroom.

"Oh," she sounded half asleep, "Hello, Bobby."

Feedback squealed deafeningly through my speakers, and all four video feeds went out, plunging my room into sudden inky darkness.

Chapter Ten

I could see the dim outline of the hallway lights around my door, and I hit it at a dead run, frantically slapping for the handle. I pulled it open and dashed into the hall and ran for 318.

I turned the ancient knob and pushed open that door with my shoulder.

The room was dark and cold again. Meghan stood between the two beds, shaking as a shadow as dark as the bottom of a grave towered over her. She didn't make a sound, but I doubt I could have heard her over the hissing whispers that filled the space. I couldn't make out a word, but I knew I didn't have a lot of time to play amateur Rosetta Stone anyway.

Full disclosure: I don't typically pick fights with the dead. I'm 0 and 1 for physical confrontations with the decidedly non-physical, which is a terrible lifetime record. But Meghan was dreadfully pale, and I couldn't tell if she was breathing. Also, I make poor decisions and I make them quickly.

I guess I figured I could disrupt the shadow and give her a chance to get some distance.

I dove through the air in what I hoped looked like a passable tackle and pitched through the center of the entity.

Expecting to pass right through and roll to my feet on the other side, I was shocked to feel myself encountering resistance. It was far from solid, but it was a tangible cold. Like sticking your hand into one of those fruit-filled Jell-O salads that used to be all the rage at potluck dinners before we all collectively admitted they were unsettling.

Except the chunks of fruit or meat were voices.

From inside the entity, I could make out the voices. Several different voices.

"She's dead already."

"He's sweating alcohol."

"We get to keep her."

"She is a better liar than anyone here."

"And we are all liars."

"We welcome her."

"He's broken."

"You can't help her, Lawrence."

"You can't help anyone."

They knew who I was. They knew a lot.

The cold came with them, locking my muscles in place and

slowing my thoughts.

Hissing into my skull they continued to whisper as their words slowly lost any meaning to me.

I completed the slow journey through the shadow and gracelessly clipped the corner of the far bed with my hip, landing in a pile of my own arms and legs. I rolled over and saw Meghan moving for the door.

She took two solid steps and fell to the carpet herself.

I fumbled in my pocket until my hand closed on the tiny LED flashlight I keep for emergencies. My jeans glowed for the half second it took me to switch it on and pull it out, turning 250 lumens of strobing light at the center of the room.

The shadow disappeared between the first strobe and the second, and I scrambled over to drag Meghan out of the room and into the hall.

She had a pulse, but it was slow and seemed weak. I'm not a doctor.

I'd wrenched my shoulder, probably when I hit the floor. I was getting entirely too much quality time with the carpet of room 318.

Spurning dignity all for the practicality of getting my injured partner out of the very public hallway, I picked Meghan up and slung her over a shoulder before dropping her on the bed in 316. I had no real reason to think whatever haunted room 318 couldn't get to us in the next room but I also hadn't seen evidence that it would.

All four video feeds were still dark. I'm sure the batteries were dead, possibly the electronics, too.

I checked Meghan again. Maybe her pulse was stronger. It just looked like she was asleep.

I couldn't see any physical injuries.

Taking her to an emergency room would be a good idea but it could wait until I knew there was something they could do for her.

I found the plastic bag with salt in it in her pocket and poured a line around the outside of the mattress. I didn't know if that would work but I wasn't going to wake her to ask. I tucked the bag back where I'd found it.

I grabbed the notepad off the desk with the Fountain House letterhead and scrawled a note:

Meghan,

I'm going downstairs to make a call. You're in a ring of salt. Call me if you wake up before I'm back.

-L

Putting the paper under a glass of ice water on the nightstand seemed the best I could do, so I made sure the door locked behind me and went downstairs.

I waved at the bartender as I arrived, and he had wordlessly poured me a whiskey before I made it to the bar.

I tipped it at him in thanks as I fished my phone out of my pocket and made my way to the patio.

For fun, I checked my flashlight. It was dead. The batteries had probably drained in about six strobes. It should have lasted for over an hour on a full charge.

I called Gloria.

She answered on the second ring. I didn't waste time with greetings.

"The entity in 318 is bad news," I told her about the shadow and, omitting details, the voices. "You've got at least a dozen things in there, and they seem aware of what's going on. It's not a repeating echo kind of thing, and it is actively hostile."

I wasn't sure I had recovered from the whispers either. Were they trying to shake my own confidence, or were they whispering with authority?

Was I 'broken'?

What would I do if I was? Nothing different, I guess.

But it wouldn't hurt to pay more attention. I was quickly getting tired of surprises.

"Well, that isn't what I wanted to hear," she sighed," but I'm glad you're alright."

"I've been tossed around a bit, but I'm fine," I didn't mention that the last time I'd technically started the confrontation and also, I had effectively hurled myself at the floor. "Meghan got hit with some kind of psychic whammy, and she's sleeping it off in my room now."

"What do you recommend we do? Is there a safe way to make the space available, or would sealing it up forever be the best move?"

"I don't know if sealing it up will work. If they figure out they can ignore doors and walls and decide they have the motivation to do so, it could get bad."

"So, can you make it safe?" he asked.

"Meghan thinks she can," I offered, "or she did anyway. She should know more once she wakes up."

"Alright. Do what you think is best," she seemed resigned," I guess there's no point in hiring an expert and then ignoring them."

"Thank you," I was actually surprised to hear that. And I was impressed. And grateful. In that order.

"One other question, Lawrence," she ventured.

"Yes?"

"Who the hell is Meghan?"

Chapter Eleven

I spend my days consulting with corporate clients and training their staff to identify potential scams, so when I tell you I was insulted by this revelation, I mean I was insulted both personally and professionally.

I told Gloria I would call her back, and I headed back upstairs. I took the elevator as my knee had complained enough earlier just going down the stairs.

My room was vacant, the glass of water empty, and the note left on the bed. There was salt everywhere.

All my belongings were there, undisturbed, so I assumed robbery wasn't a motivation. Not that there's a huge secondary market for ghost-hunting gear and business casual earth tones.

I went into the bathroom to splash water on my face. The battered face looking back at me from the mirror looked like he'd seen the bad sides of several bar fights. He favored his wounded leg even just standing there on a level tile floor, the opposite shoulder hanging loosely.

I moved my arm. It wasn't dislocated, but the bruising made holding it in the proper position uncomfortable.

This hunt had gone wrong before Meghan showed up, but I

still wanted to find an excuse to blame her.

But the truth is, as much as I hated to admit it, I had been at an impasse before she lied her way into this investigation.

What bothered me was not knowing why she even wanted to be involved. I hadn't advertised my activity and Gloria Anderson had chosen to not hire a local resource, probably as an attempt at discretion.

If Meghan hadn't faked a connection to Gloria, I wouldn't have for a moment entertained the thought of allowing her to poke at restless, dead things with me.

Maybe, on some level, I knew I was in over my head. Possibly I'd spent so much time nursing temporary relationships for work between rounds of hanging out with my cat at home it had left me in need of some human connection.

Maybe catching a heavy glass ashtray with my face early on just impaired my judgment.

Whatever her motivation had been, her connection with Beau Neumann and his entanglements with Austin's polite society had given this investigation a direction that, prior to her involvement, had been entirely rudderless.

I decided if I saw her again, I wouldn't yell at her.

I could keep this professional. I'd been duped but I wasn't

necessarily worse off for it.

She had pulled me out of a nasty situation, too.

I think I had returned the favor earlier that evening.

I grabbed a plastic cup out of the bathroom and filled it halfway from my dwindling bottle of whiskey. I didn't bother running down the hallway for ice.

I looked over at the darkened screens of the monitors crowded onto the tiny hotel room desk and tried to figure out where the evening had gone wrong.

She did the sage and the quartz and the salt stuff, but I was still on the fence about what exactly that even meant. If I was willing to believe it made a difference, it kind of changed my whole scientific equation. I had enough trouble earning credibility from my haunted clientele with my tried-and-true scientific approach. If I had to sell some witchy nonsense to the straights, I'd probably need to actually believe it on some level.

She had been expecting Anne-Marie, but she had greeted Bobby before everything went south.

I didn't know what that meant either, but I was sure it meant something.

Anne-Marie had been murdered in the room. She had every reason to still be upset about it.

Whether she was cheating on her soon-to-be husband or intending to destroy his criminal family, her life wasn't headed in the direction she had expected at the time she died.

"What have you done to me?" The voice had asked. Was she asking about being shot, or had that been Bobby asking about disloyalty?

I leafed through my pen and paper notes.

Bobby Rose felt he had been betrayed, but he allegedly suspected infidelity and not that his fiancée was working with the feds.

Either way, he had had a very bad day. Was that enough for his own family to have him killed in a fake escape attempt?

Having had my own share of bad days, I felt a moment of sympathy for my booze-running, kneecap-busting, pimping, long-dead new friend.

That moment was harshly interrupted when I heard a woman scream in terror through my shared wall with room 318.

I had never heard her scream, but I recognized Meghan's voice.

She had gone back in there, and I hadn't even thought to check.

I burst into room 318 with no idea what was going on and

absolutely no plan in place, but I was greeted by chaos, which would have derailed the meticulous instructions for an Ikea bookcase anyway.

Dark shapes revolved around Meghan's huddled form on the floor, whispering again in a bony chatter.

The drapes flew outward as though driven by some phantom hurricane winds I couldn't feel.

Four pillows seemed to launch themselves against the wall over the table, holding the television to bounce and scatter across the carpet.

Rhythmically, the bathroom door opened, banged against the interior wall, then slammed closed again like a demented Morse code.

I went to grab Meghan to drag her towards the door again, but that door slammed shut, and the deadbolt threw itself into place as soon as I stepped away from it. I'd worry about that when I was ready to leave.

Both mattresses jumped up and outward to pin themselves against opposite walls, blasting the room with the smell of copper and gunpowder and exposing the water-stained box springs decades past the normal lifespans of hotel furniture.

I stooped to try to grab Meghan under her arms and passed

through one of the spinning shadows. The whispers were just inarticulate screaming. Even with the icy cold, I preferred it to the last conversation.

As I went to start moving back towards the door, the nightstand skittered across the floor and slammed into my back, knocking me forward and into the far wall. The lamp and clock radio clattered to the floor in a tangle, and I caught a glimpse of that old ashtray rolling under the bed closest to the front door.

I grabbed Meghan's wrist and started to drag her and myself towards the hope of that locked front door. As I turned to look that way, I saw that enormous dark form filling the entryway between us and our only exit.

It breathed slowly and wetly, swelling and looming over us. Even if we could squeeze past it, it swayed back and forth erratically, fading back and then stepping solidly forward.

Meghan was unresponsive. Her eyes were locked in place, staring at something I couldn't see. If I'd had to guess, I'd have bet whatever she was looking at was worse than what I was.

And what I turned to look at was an enormous shadow slowly moving closer and closer to where I was crouched on the floor, trying to hover over my catatonic partner.

Desperately, I patted her down in the dark and found the

plastic bag of salt. I pulled it out and slung the contents in an arc in front of us, interrupting the entity into a dispersing cloud of darkness.

I fumbled with the deadbolt and the ancient doorknob, both cold enough to make my fingers stick, and got the door open, dragging Meghan out and onto the hallway carpet before letting the door slam shut behind us.

I absently heard the deadbolt latch again and lay on the floor with my eyes closed, trying to get my breathing back under control.

Meghan made a soft, whimpering kind of noise next to me, and I turned to look at her.

We were surrounded by dead children.

Chapter Twelve

I had heard stories of ghostly children in the hotel before I had arrived, but I tend to discount those.

Children rarely have the kind of grievances that result in a tormented, lingering spirit. Thankfully.

But you've surely heard the ghost stories of the sounds of a child's laughter and the echoes of pattering feet. It's almost a cliche at this point in our folkloric history.

One of the miraculous things about these sounds is that residual hauntings don't involve an actual tortured soul. It's the repeating sound of a human emotion. There are few sounds in the mortal world that can hold a tenth of the joy as the sound of an untroubled child laughing and playing.

It leaves a mark on a place even, and especially, if that child later grew up and lived a full and contented life.

This wasn't that. This wasn't that at all.

The dozen or so children surrounding Meghan and I were engaged in various activities.

A pair of boys seemed to be playing with invisible marbles on the hallway floor. Another girl sat with her back to the wall, looking like she was quietly reading a book I couldn't see.

All around us, children were amusing themselves silently in the hallway as though they had always been there. Or maybe it was just that they thought they always had.

They could have been mistaken for historical reenactors dragged to an event by their nerdy parents if all the children hadn't shared the same glossy, pitch-black eyes. Eyes which, pair by pair, turned to focus on us.

Meghan rolled over and pushed herself up into a sitting position, her head swiveling around to take in the sight of our new visitors.

A little girl behind us cradled what looked like an empty doll-sized blanket. A boy who looked about eight years old gestured for a dog I couldn't see to be quiet as his gaze never left us.

Their cherubic faces lacked any color of health, settling on a dull gray instead. On closer inspection, they all wore clothes soiled by dirt or worse and sported mussed hair. The tidiest little girl had what looked like at one time, long ago, had been the suggestion of braids.

Blackened lips peeled back across jagged teeth.

"I used the last of your salt," I confessed quietly, "It'd be nice if you had some other trick."

Meghan focused on the two little boys closest to us and just watched them for a moment. "Hello, children," she pitched her voice higher into that sing-song cadence kids seem to like, but that crawls up my spine like a handful of soft-serve spiders, "Why are you all up past your bedtimes?"

I shifted to get my uninjured knee under me and calculated the amount of time it would take to get to my room. It had probably locked behind me, as hotel rooms do. I'd have to get past at least six of the little undead urchins and that was just if the rest didn't rush me when I moved.

The other direction I could get to the unlocked stairwell, maybe. It was a longer run, and it would take me a lot closer to even more of these things.

Neither option was appealing.

"I can tell you one more bedtime story," she offered," but then you all have to go to bed, alright?"

I had tensed to grab Meghan and launch myself towards the stairwell when I saw the little girl holding the phantom doll, slowly nodding her head.

Looking around, I could see that she wasn't the only one.

There was no way this was going to work. I looked back at Meghan. She had shifted into a cross-legged pose, her body language relaxed.

"I'm going to share a very old story with you all," she leaned forward as the children started to shuffle over, "but it is one of my very favorites."

You know the original Grimm versions of fairy tales? With the gruesome endings and all the gore and mutilations? Those stories obviously commissioned by Big Parent back in the days before CPS and child psychologists just to keep kids from wandering into the woods?

Those are my personal favorites.

Meghan went with a very toned-down Goldilocks and the Three Bears. She even wrapped it up before the bears ate Goldilocks at the end.

That is how it ends, right? Is that just the German version? Even as a child I felt that it was justified.

As she completed her story, the children faded away one by one. The last little boy waved goodbye at her and walked into the wall across from my room.

He passed out of sight, and I relaxed muscles I hadn't remembered tensing.

"Nicely done," I started, "how did you know that would work?"

"I didn't," she unfolded herself and offered me a hand up.

I didn't take it.

She pressed on, "I just knew I needed to try something before you went for one of your flying tackles on a child."

"Not a child," I stressed, "a ghost. A bunch of ghosts."

Why was I defensive? I hadn't even planned to tackle anything. I was just going to grab her and run away. Thank you very much.

"Why did you lie to me?" I didn't sound as angry as I could have, "How did you even know there was an investigation here? And how did you know who I was and where to find me? Who the hell even are you, really?"

I may have sounded a little angrier at the end. It had been a long night.

"Can we not do this in the hallway?" She glanced around.

"If anyone comes along, you can just tell them a bedtime story," I shook my head, "but don't skip the murdery parts this time."

I unlocked my door and stepped inside the room, turning and holding up a finger in Meghan's direction while I slipped inside and grabbed my bottle of whiskey.

The bar downstairs was closed by that time and there was no way I was having this discussion sober.

Wordlessly, we walked to the elevator and rode down in silence.

I grabbed two glasses off the drying mat at the end of the bar and walked us back to the fireplace with its dwindling fire. The main lights had been shut off, so the room was painted in deep orange firelight and long shadows.

I set both glasses on the side table and poured generously into both. I set down the bottle and eased back into one of the armchairs.

"Well?" I handed her the other glass, "Start with whichever question you want, but start."

I used the look I reserve for executives who fall for phishing scams. It's generally pretty effective.

Meghan took an extended sip of room-temperature whiskey, followed by a deep breath.

"A ghost told me," She looked down, "a ghost told me in a dream that death would follow this investigation."

"It follows everything. That's how death works." I wrapped my hands around my glass, "What ghost?"

"Judith Mounier," she took a deep breath as though mustering her resolve, "She said I needed to find you, and she said you'd be in the bar alone, and you were."

"To be fair, that's just statistically likely for me," I was still unsettled.

"I know you aren't really a big believer," she poured herself another couple of fingers of whiskey, "but when I have one of these dreams, they don't lie. Judith visited me the night you got that bruise. She said it would get worse, and she was right about that, too."

"Wait, we haven't even seen Judith," I really wasn't sure who we had seen. It had all been looming shapes and shadows to me, "Have you seen Judith?"

She shook her head, "Not since I got here. It's possible she is one of the shadows in 318, but the big looming one you threw the salt at definitely was not Judith."

"Okay," she had opened another line of questioning for me, so I went with it, "Why salt? What does that do?"

"Scientifically?" She asked, "I don't know. It's not like there's a ghost lab at MIT where they study this stuff. The theory is that salt is Of The Earth," I could hear the capitalization, "and spirits are not Of The Earth, so it repels them. I just know that it works for some reason."

"I'll add it to the shopping list," and I meant it. I couldn't debate that it had been effective for whatever reason. "So, who was the big shadow? Bobby, right? You greeted Bobby just before all my equipment went dark.”

“I saw a young man,” her eyes seemed to glaze over a bit, as though she were seeing him again, “I didn’t see him become the big shadow, but that makes sense. Maybe he looks different when he’s manifesting to move something in the room.”

“Or to attack,” I amended.

“So,” the word was heavy, “am I off the case?”

I looked at her in the dying light.

“No. But if you lie to me again, next time, I’ll just let something dark and evil murder you.”

She knew I was telling a lie myself. I’m very bad at it.

After calling a ride, Meghan went home, and I retreated to my room. The hallway was mercifully free of spectral children.

I would never have considered a bedtime story. She had been correct. I suppose Plan B would have involved tackling. Maybe that’s why my friends never ask me to babysit.

Yeah. That’s it.

I drank the last of the whiskey without bothering with a glass and fell into a fitful sleep.

I'm on a quiet cul-de-sac, looking at the front of a comfortably worn house. Walking up the front steps, I can't help but look up at the beadboard ceiling over the small front porch. It's covered in spiderwebs and abandoned wasp nests.

It's light blue. Powdery blue. Like the memory of a robin's egg.

It's haint blue. A milk and lye-based paint pigmented with indigo and formulated to look like the open sky. You see it in the southeast over porches and entryways.

Tradition says it confuses evil spirits, so they drift off before entering a home.

I go inside and know it doesn't work.

There are shadowy figures in the hallway to the left. I ignore them.

I pour a drink and sit in the old armchair by the backdoor.

I know I'm waiting for something, but I can't remember what. Or who.

I also don't remember pouring another drink, but my glass is still full when the last light of the setting sun illuminates the foyer, and my eyes are drawn to the front door.

A man walks from the dark hallway across the entryway and disappears behind the wall towards the garage entrance.

He's tall but still has the ruddy look of youth. He's wearing a white shirt and dark trousers with a stripe down the outside of the leg, and well-worn boots.

I don't know who he is or why he is here, but I know that he is dead.

He's here every day. He's been here longer than I have.

He'll be here when I'm gone. It feels like I already am.

Chapter Thirteen

I grew up in a tiny West Texas town with a population of around three thousand, and almost half of that was willing to admit it on government forms.

Don't get me wrong, we had a proud history around breakfast cereal going back to the days when there was cocaine in it and an honestly thriving arts community aggressively reclaiming the dead or dying downtown area.

I heard they got an actual McDonald's (after my family moved away) to compete with both the Dairy Queen and the locally owned off-brand Dairy Kween.

While we may not have had a suspiciously constantly broken soft serve machine, what we did have was local history and folklore.

The story of the town's founding was centered on an East Coast breakfast drink magnate deciding to create a utopia in the West Texas desert based on higher education, upward mobility, and the fact that coffee was evil.

"Super weird that this didn't catch on," said absolutely no one who has ever had a cup of coffee.

It was the kind of place I could ride my bike all over at any time of the day or night with no fear of human predators. Or maybe that was just a hallmark of the era.

There were sightings of all kinds of things in the canyons surrounding the town. Humanoid figures, dog-like animals that walked on two feet, and visions of the founder of the town in his second-floor window, even though his eventual suicide was technically in California, were commonplace, discussed openly among the children of the town, and confirmed by whatever adults were around.

It was an accepted part of living there, a part of the frontier spirit of the place, I guess.

Buffalo Point on the Macy Ranch was a cliff where the natives drove buffalo to their deaths as part of their hunt long before the white man showed up. There are still bones at the bottom of that cliff face and pictographs of those hunts and, eventually, the arrival of wagon trains. Locals report that on certain nights, you can see spectral herds of bison run over the edge of the cliff and plunge into the darkness.

I was at a friend's house one weekend when his uncle, who worked out in the oil fields, explained how his truck got damaged.

He was leaving the job site at sundown a few days previous along a hard-packed dirt road when something came out of the brush and attacked him. The bottom half of a horse and the top half of a large, bald-headed man. It kept pace with the Ford for at least a mile, pounding his fists into the side panels of the truck and bellowing in rage.

The man had never heard of a centaur, but the mythological creature met the description perfectly.

I think everyone was unsettled by that conversation.

We also had our very own witch story. Miss Sarah was our resident witch, and she was buried outside Terrace Cemetery, the only public cemetery in the county. And she rested outside of it in a horse pasture because, as the townsfolk knew, she was a witch. What with all the crop cursing and livestock blighting so, it was pretty obvious that she had made a pact with the devil. I mean, trying to grow crops and raise livestock in a literal desert could, hypothetically, be difficult, but there was a woman to blame, so that's the direction they went in.

In 1920, Miss Sarah was buried way out in this field under a simple marker and quickly faded into the tapestry of local folklore.

By the time I got to high school, the witch story was at its apex. If you walked out into the field after dark and touched her grave marker and then made it back to your car to escape, Miss Sarah would grant your wish. She had been buried apart from everyone else so that when the devil came for her soul, he wouldn't accidentally grab the soul of one of the decent folk.

It was a childish, uneducated drivel, but in an attempt to hang out with the cool kids, I participated more than once. I don't remember any specific wish I had at the time.

I had a class project in my high school freshman year to document something from local history, and I really wanted to expose our own local witch trials, but what I found in the newspaper archives was way less fun than I had expected.

Miss Sarah was simply the only black person to die in the town during the time when segregation was legal. She was buried alone in the black section of the cemetery, which no longer existed.

When I say I face horrors, I know I am not alone in that. And I know, at the end of the day, I can ditch my equipment and walk away.

I have an easier path than most. I won't ever forget that.

Chapter Fourteen

Oakwood Cemetery is the oldest public cemetery in Austin. It was originally situated on a remote hilltop in the 1850s, but now it is surrounded by a city with a great view of downtown if you happen to be at an altitude above six feet under.

Legend states the first "residents" were the victims of a Comanche raid, but if those graves exist, they aren't marked.

It's a protected historic landmark in view of the state capital, but that hasn't shielded it from the trappings of modern urban decline.

As I stepped through the iron gates just unlocked by the groundskeepers for sunrise, I immediately took note of the vast assortment of grave markers.

There are some simple stones flush with the surrounding grass and huge mausoleums. Traditional standing stones with graceful, curved tops or crosses or angels sit in clusters arranged by family in some places and in sedimentary layers laid out by the era of their internment.

Graffiti marked more fence stones than not, and empty beer cans and bottles lay scattered around the grounds.

An enormous, spray-painted tag marred the inside of the

cemetery fence across the stone base. I couldn't make out what it said, but penmanship doesn't apply to spray can work.

Cemetery fences are amazing things. This one was eight feet tall and topped with pointed decorative finials, but it obviously hadn't kept anyone out. But that isn't what cemetery fences are for.

Our first assumption is that cemetery fences are to protect the dead, but the dead are beyond protecting. These fences, most often made of iron, aren't designed to keep anyone out. They exist as a demarcation for the dead. As a separation from the living. It makes us feel better that there is a boundary that separates us from death, however decorative that boundary may be.

The Egyptians used the Nile the same way – Living on the east and the dead on the west. It's in our DNA.

There was a used hypodermic needle on a bench next to what I'd guessed was a discarded t-shirt.

I found some of the Bertrands in a little area near the entrance. The dates were in the neighborhood, but there was no marker for Anne-Marie. I could have had the wrong branch of the family tree, or maybe she wasn't interred there at all. I knew I'd have to speak with an attendant.

The problem with that is that for a famous person, which Anne-Marie qualified as due to the ghost stories written up in various books and haunted tours, the attendant would assume I was up to no good.

I wasn't really at Oakwood for Anne-Marie anyway. I scanned the stones and started walking for the oldest-looking ones. The uphill portion of the cemetery held the oldest markers, but I was surprised to see the dew-wet grass pressed down in a straight line in front of me. These graves had already had at least one visitor this morning.

I was dressed for work, so I wouldn't look too out of place if I encountered an actual mourner.

The stones were increasingly degraded by time as I moved deeper into the graveyard along the trail blazed by the other early morning visitor. I had begun to think I couldn't read the stones to find what I was looking for, even if I stumbled across it when I saw a large, rusted iron archway over the entrance for an area with a waist-high fence around it. The top of the arch read "Rose."

There were twenty or so markers in the little area, all made of weathered marble. The latest date of death was in the 1950s, back on the eastern edge of the plot. The further west I went, the older and harder to read the stones became.

On the far western side, there was a cracked gravestone that was too weathered to read the carving. The top had broken off at some point and had been propped up against the remaining vertical bit.

There were odd red squiggly marks brushed across both pieces of the monument alongside the initials RR. It was the only marker in the area with flowers on it, but they were dried and crumbling. Black candlewax rivulets flowed down the face of the stone, and there was a shallow hole dug just in front of the base like a divot on a polo pitch.

I took pictures of everything and texted them to Meghan, relieved for once to have another side of the street to throw things at. It looked occult to me, but unless it was set dressing on Buffy the Vampire Slayer, I wouldn't stand a chance at identifying anything.

On sending the last photo, I noticed the fresh footpath I'd been following led right up to the other side of the metal fence from RR before heading away towards the north side of the cemetery, opposite the entrance. I had a sudden urge to find out why someone else would have an interest in this hundred-year-old grave.

I hopped over the fence like an idiot and felt a jolt of pain from my injured leg. I sucked a quick breath between my clamped teeth and started off on the trail of the mystery mourner. The sun was starting to bake the moisture off the grass so if I was going to follow this trail, I needed to do it before it evaporated totally.

I hustled down the hill, past more and more recent graves, when I spotted a small form cutting left around some trees, obstructing my view.

I took off towards the left and down in an attempt to intercept. As I rounded a mausoleum, I glimpsed a young girl in a short skirt, hoodie, and leather jacket slip between the bars on the north fence and hop into the passenger side of a silver pickup truck, which immediately merged into traffic and headed downtown.

Tracking down a specific silver pickup anywhere in Texas would be effectively impossible without a license plate, fingerprints, and DNA from the driver. There were just too many on the roads.

I turned to walk back uphill while I watched them fade into the distance and almost immediately fell into the dark bottom of a freshly dug, open grave.

Chapter Fifteen

I stayed conscious and regretted that immediately.

I had vaguely caught myself with my bad shoulder and landed on my bum knee. I was covered in mud and tweed, and a clump of sod had followed me into the grave only to land on my neck and shoulder.

I heaved myself out of the hole and stood up, trying to brush the muck off my clothes with minimal success.

On the way back to the Fountain House, I called my client and told them I wasn't feeling well and would be working from the hotel that day. It wasn't totally a lie – I didn't feel well. I felt like I'd fallen into one.

And I had paperwork to catch up on anyway, so working from the room would honestly let me complete my deliverables for the week.

Around mid-afternoon, I texted Meghan again and asked her to meet me at the Iron Cactus after work, I realized I'd been in Austin for days without having a single nacho, and I didn't want to risk getting deported from Texas for unpatriotic activities.

She replied that she was running down a lead and would be there as soon as possible, probably around six.

I patiently waited in the bar area of the Iron Cactus reverse image, searching for the strange glyphs I'd seen at the Rose family plot. They must have been painted on the headstone with an accent because I had no luck.

What I did have was two frozen margaritas the size of my head before Meghan showed up. I told her about what happened after I sent her the pictures, and she stifled a laugh.

"You're lucky the situation wasn't more grave," she said, barely hiding her grin behind a hand.

"Your sympathy warms me, Meghan."

"At least you can't be accused of losing the plot," she shook with laughter.

There was not enough guacamole in the world to make me not regret my open honesty.

"It's just so sad when a parapsychologist buries himself in his work, Lair," I thought she might be having trouble breathing.

"Some of us care about the plight of the terrestrially bound, Meghan," I said flatly.

She placed her napkin on the table and rocked back, staring at the ceiling. "Did you just suggest that 'terrestrially bound Americans' are a protected class?"

"Don't make me pitch myself into a hole to protest your

bigotry against the life challenged, Meghan," I was determinedly assembling a fajita and attempting to not collapse into laughter.

Ultimately, we both abandoned our attempts to keep a straight face. It felt nice to laugh, even if it was at my own expense. I mean, I know that guy, and he's asking for it.

"That's why you're a Lair, you know," she mopped at spilled queso on the vinyl table cover, "If you don't joke about your trauma, you'd have to really process it. So you say ridiculous things to distract yourself from it."

Not cracking another joke just then was physically painful.

"It's your lair, don't you see? Your refuge from whatever hurts you."

I did see. And I didn't much care for it.

"I had no luck searching for whatever was painted on RR's grave," I offered, "I checked the standard occult boards and wiccan symbols."

"Yeah, that makes sense," she had just loaded her own tortilla with chicken and brilliantly doused it with the table salsa, "It's not your standard witchy glyphs."

It looked like there was enough salsa left for me to duplicate her fajita, and fajita plagiarism isn't a thing, so that's what I did, "Any idea what it actually is?"

"I know someone in linguistics at the University," she explained, "It's Ogham script," she said it like 'OW-uhm', "Druid tree writing. It's pre-Roman."

"What does it mean?" I asked.

"Every character is a type of plant, but they all have alternate meanings," she finished her fajita, "This particular sequence means 'renewed life.'"

"That doesn't sound too sinister," I waved for another cranium-sized margarita.

"On its own, it's not," she said, "but if it is written as a decree and not a history, it crosses some metaphysical lines."

"Do you think someone was trying to bring back Bobby?" This was even more new territory for me. I hate new territory.

"You mean like an actual, physical body? There wouldn't be much left at this point, and it's impossible, anyway," She shook her head, "You're really warming up to the spooky, aren't you?"

"No," I clarified, "but I have seen things I can't dismiss, and I don't think a laser grid and a digital voice recorder will help out a whole lot here."

"My theory is that this is all about the missing dirt," she scrolled over to the photo showing the divot in front of the headstone. "Graveyard dirt has uses in traditional spell work."

"Oh, so now we're skipping right to witches and magic?" I mention one resurrection ritual and all of the sudden, I'm Dick Sargent. Or, more likely, Dick York.

"I'm just saying," she didn't sound defensive at all and was, in fact, going for more salsa, "In traditional magic, graveyard dirt from the grave of a loved one is used for protection or for love and prosperity spells."

"And dirt from the grave of a murdering career criminal?"

"Not love or protection," she shuddered, "dark works. Curses, hexes . . . Death magic."

"Okay. That's less pleasant."

She nodded, "It's also a good way to rile up an already restless spirit. Think about it – his fiancée betrays him, and his family abandons or possibly murders him, and then some misguided idiot goes and steals from his grave?"

"Yeah, it's enough to make you want to check into a hotel and try to murder the poor sap in the next room a hundred years later."

Chapter Sixteen

We listened at the door of room 318 and heard nothing. You know how they tell you if the building is on fire, you should check the doorknob for heat to determine if the room on the other side is burning? I did that but checked it for cold. It was hallway temperature.

I unlocked the door and swung it open. The room had been put back together, the mattresses back in place, and the furniture reset. The beds were even made, and the drapes were tucked into their brackets, letting in the gentle glow of the city at night. Room 318 was specifically left off the rotation for housekeeping.

That ashtray was back on the nightstand.

Meghan stepped into the room as I gathered up my equipment. It needed to be checked, and the batteries had to be replaced, but there was no sense in doing that in 318.

"Anything?" I asked her.

"No," her eyes were half closed, and her arms outstretched, "There was a lot of energy expended last time. Maybe the entities needed a night off?"

"I know I could use one," I was feeling more and more like the dead myself.

I hauled the gear back to my room and dropped everything on the bed. I began testing batteries.

They were all dead. A couple of the nine volts had split at the seams and leaked acid, but I hoped it wasn't enough to damage the electronics.

I set about cleaning and testing everything while Meghan stood behind me, her hand pressed to the common wall with 318.

I had just started checking the video quality on the second camera when she patted her bag and walked into the hallway. She was back before I finished checking the third. There was no degradation in the quality of the video. I was relieved.

"So, what is the path forward?" She asked.

The week had more than caught up with me. "Tomorrow is Friday," I looked at the calendar on my phone for no particular reason, "I plan to call my cat sitter in the morning and extend this trip through the weekend."

"I figured you for a dog person," she seemed to reassess me on the spot.

"I travel too much to have a dog," I said, "and Aengus appreciates his alone time."

"Aengus?" She raised an eyebrow.

"The shelter called him Stephen, but that didn't suit him," I brushed off the question, "What are the chances we can have this place safe for visitors by Sunday night, in your opinion?"

She put her hand back against the wall, "Not great. It's possible, but there are a lot of moving pieces now."

"Yeah, we've got vengeful spirits, familial murder, an honest-to-god criminal empire, and now someone hijacking grave dirt."

"And the ghost kids," she added, "I'm not sure how they are connected to this, if they even are."

"Okay," I offered, "so we meet back here tomorrow night, and you can help me rewire 318 for surveillance. Then what?"

"Then I ask some questions, and we try to get a lead on our cemetery visitor, I guess."

"I don't have a better idea," I admitted.

I walked Meghan to the elevator and said goodnight. When I turned to return to my room, I noticed an addition to the side table at the end of the hallway.

Meghan had left a stack of construction paper and a jumbled pile of crayons.

I didn't touch them.

I'm again on a quiet cul-de-sac, looking at the front of a comfortably worn house. Walking up the front steps, I can't help but look up at the beadboard ceiling over the small front porch. It's covered in spiderwebs and abandoned wasp nests.

It's light blue. Powdery blue. Like the memory of a robin's egg.

It's haint blue. You see it in the southeast over porches and entryways.

I enter the house and cut left down the darkened hallway.

The guest bathroom is empty, but the front bedroom is filled with whispers.

I turn right and enter the master suite. Thick layers of dark red paint on the walls still bleed through with the sickly yellow of years gone by. My desk sits dark. A breaker probably tripped earlier in the day for no diagnosable reason. In the far corner, a small figure stands next to the nightstand near my side of the bed.

He's about two feet tall, reddish, with a cherubic belly and feet like a crane. He has a bulbous nose and a too-wide smile that doesn't reach the soulless pits of his eyes.

He bounces from foot to foot and claps his hands at me eagerly.

"Whatever," I walk to the dining room to pour a drink before

heading to the garage to deal with the spider-infested breaker box.

99

Chapter Seventeen

Dawn came early, as it seems to do when I skip regular sleep for a few days in a row. Or when tequila shots are the nightly special. It's not my fault I'm fiscally responsible.

I stared at the increasingly battered man in the mirror of the tiny hotel bathroom and decided that while he looked like he'd been dragged through hell, he also looked like he was ready to go back to file a formal complaint.

Or maybe he was crazy. The guy had an obvious head injury. Why don't we just go easy on him?

After a trip to a hardware store for batteries and assorted supplies, I went to work to close out my week. I turned in my paperwork, administered a training class for a few groups of users, and knocked off early to sneak in a nap.

I had a feeling it was going to be a long night. I was used to working alone, to being alone.

But sometimes, life or the universe or whatever complicates things by adding other people to your carefully curated equation. Math on the fly isn't my thing. Math at all really isn't my thing.

Maybe it's the concept of something being meant to be that gives me pause. I tend to think what happens is the result of our choices. That could be empowering, I suppose, but for me it's the thought that keeps me awake when I should be sleeping.

If every awful thing I've seen is my fault, then I've made some truly horrible decisions in my life.

If things are just meant to be, then there's not anything I can do about it. It's too easy for that to be correct.

But I had another stop to make, and brooding over loss and trauma and the past in general was just another excuse to put it off.

I stepped into the shadowy interior of The Cauldron - a tiny bookstore around a corner from the university.

It was packed with books on an assortment of subjects. Religions, both active and ancient, auras, divination, and spell books, that apparently come in glossy paperback editions these days, which must save the publisher tons of money on human skin.

The air was thick with incense, and every surface not crammed full of books was cluttered with crystals, little statues, ritual tools I could only vaguely identify, and candles.

I was reading the placard in front of a pile of orange candles only because it was the first on the right, and I needed a methodology when a young woman walked up behind me and asked if she could help.

She was very short, maybe five feet, with short spiky hair

dyed an oddly vibrant lavender even in the dim light of the candle section. She wore sandals, jeans, and a black t-shirt for what I assumed was a local band.

"I honestly don't know," I answered, "I guess I'm looking for some protection?"

She peered at me for a moment through a thick set of glasses with rims heavy enough to make me wonder if they could be considered goggles. Do goggles require a strap, or is that all about the protective lens?

"I'll say you are," she reached out with a tattooed arm and touched my left hand, closed her eyes, and took a deep breath. "Oh, he's following you. He's very upset that he didn't kill you."

"Well, I'm seeing him later, and he's going to probably try again," What was with this town? "Can you recommend something to, I don't know, take the spiritual edge off?"

She looked puzzled.

I muscled on, "We tried salt with good effect. So maybe some kind of extra-strength salt?"

"You've got a ghost here in town?" she was catching on.

"Yeah," I answered, "my partner and I are investigating a local hotel, and it's more aggressive than I would like. I'm just trying to cover my bases."

She shouldered past me and grabbed some candles, a plastic bag that looked like something I'd find in the locker of one of the cooler kids in my high school, and a brass bell and dropped them all into a handbasket, which she held out towards me. "This should tone down whatever your ghost is doing. Sage candles, mugwort, and if you get into trouble, ring the bell. It will disrupt negative spiritual activity."

I moved to take the handle of the basket, "that sounds easy enough," I smiled at her in thanks.

She didn't let go of the basket. In fact, she closed her right hand over my own on the handle.

"This is fine for ghosts," she leaned forward, "but it won't help you with who is following you. He's marked you. He has been following you. For years."

Her eyes brimmed with tears.

"Wait," I was lost, "What?"

"I can feel his shadow on you," she said, "it's so cold."

I needed a drink.

"I'll take it under advisement," I answered, "I just need to get this ghost situation under control right now. I appreciate your help."

She took another long look at me; her gaze was telescopic.

"Hornsby Bend," she gave me a weak smile, "You need to see it while you're here."

"Thanks, I will. Can you check me out?" I asked, hefting the basket I was now the only one holding.

"Oh," she wiped at her eyes and turned for the door, "I don't work here."

She went out the door and disappeared down the sidewalk.

The Hornsby Bend Bird Observatory is a 1200-acre wastewater treatment site just southeast of Austin proper. It's also the host to very dense urban biodiversity, recycling and composting research, and countless environmental surveys. It's also a top spot for bird-watching tourism, which is apparently a thing that exists.

They even produce an EPA-certified soil conditioner called Dillo Dirt™.

Texas, am I right?

Woods and grasslands hug a lazy point in the Colorado River, and it is possible to think you've traveled back to pre-frontier times if you don't turn around to see the Austin skyline peeking through the dense foliage.

Hiking trails wind their way across the reserve, and natural clearings lend themselves to gatherings of bird watchers, Austin hippies, and, as it turns out, a local enclave of modern druids and witches. They are all probably technically pretty much the same people in most of the ways that matter.

I followed the trails for a bit, but my dress shoes were woefully inappropriate for that. They grew more useless as I finally wandered off the trail and edged towards the river.

Eventually, the mud sucked them one by one away. I didn't even notice when I lost my soaked and mud-crusted socks as well.

I wandered into a glade with only a thin stand of live oaks between me and the river. Narrow live oak acorns scattered across the ground in decaying piles. Waist-high switchgrass sprawled across a nature-salvaged meadow before me.

At the center of the space, reclaimed poles of local wood were arranged in a loose circle, the bottoms only just beginning to rot from the damp. The glade smelled of pine pollen and low river and squirrels and ceremony.

I wondered if the poles were some part of the bird observatory. Could they have been erected as nesting sites or roosting perches or . . . I honestly couldn't think of what use a bird would have for standing wooden poles in a clearing. I'm not a bird guy.

The one thing that all cat people and all dog people can

universally agree on is that bird people are weird.

I heard an owl call out into the sunlit clearing. As a rule, I don't go outside often. I work with computers. And outside is where we keep the bugs.

But owl noises in daylight triggered some primal fear in me. It was unexpected, sure, but it was also unnatural.

But then I heard worse.

I heard an inhuman shriek from back in the trees. A mourning wail that shook me and made me notice the cold mud between my toes.

It held sorrow and it held loss, and it held grim inevitability. And it projected them all across that simple, open woodland glade.

I watched a hooded figure dart between the trees lining the river, a long, tattered cloak trailing behind her.

She shrieked again, and I thought of every memorial service I'd ever attended, every funeral for a loved one, every moment of silence at the Oscars for someone who had partied just a bit too hard the year before.

I couldn't help it. It consumed me.

Death was coming, and she was absolutely not going to be taking a number or waiting on hold for the next available representative.

Chapter Eighteen

I borrowed a luggage cart from my new, totally best friend Thad at the front desk and lugged all my new supplies up to my room before I called Gloria. Practically, she needed to know I'd still be camping out in room 316. But more, I needed to tell her that we would do what we could but had a Sunday deadline.

Personally, I could probably spend six months just recording data in the famously haunted room 318, but I had a cat to get home to, and the part of the investigations Gloria was interested in, namely the assurance of safety for her potential guests, would be complete by Sunday or beyond our abilities.

My planned nap eluded me, as the truly important naps seem to do.

I kept hearing vague noises from 318 that seemed to require immediate identification.

The occasional "THUMP-drag" could be written off as luggage being moved by a living human in another nearby room.

Muted voices could similarly be written off as my fellow hotel guests going about their lives, deciding what to put on the TV or where to go for dinner.

But some part of my possibly ashtray-damaged brain still

interpreted it as falling corpses and accusations of betrayal.

Just as the daylight started to fade on the blinds in my hotel window there was a sharp knock at the door.

I opened it to see Meghan, her expression strained and her face white.

"We need to talk," she said, "downstairs, ten minutes."

She spun and headed for the stairwell, a bundle pressed against her chest like precious cargo.

Ten minutes. Fine.

I've dressed more quickly for worse reasons, but tonight, I was going in uniform.

I traded my jeans for black cargo pants and my flannel for a long-sleeved black thermal shirt and a vest loaded with pockets. I considered my canvas Israeli combat boots but, at the last minute, opted to keep the black cowboy boots. This was still Texas. Sometimes you've just got to represent, you know?

I did the standard pocket transfer – wallet, keys, breath mints, and added digital voice recorders, a laser thermometer, and two EMF detectors to the pockets blossoming across my chest.

I'd bought a 25-pound bin of driveway salt at the hardware store, but I didn't break that open yet.

I also didn't bother with setting up video recording and all my data gathering.

We would set things right, or we would fail terribly, and all the analysis in the world after it was over would be meaningless.

I took the elevator down to the lobby and sat down at the bar next to Meghan.

At a wave, the bartender delivered a glass of whiskey. It was late afternoon, so I didn't feel a lot of judgment from the room. Or maybe I'm immune to that by now.

"I picked these up this afternoon," Meghan said, placing a stack of construction paper in front of me.

The top sheet had faint lines in crayon on its face, depicting a man in black wearing what looked like a cowboy hat.

"Wait," I looked closer, taking note of the bow tie the man in the drawing was wearing and the enormous gun in his right hand, "You don't mean to imply the kids from the hallway did this?"

"On the third floor, the only other tenants are two couples staying at the ends of the hallway," she clarified, "and neither checked in with kids."

"Yeah, but we don't know ghosts actually played with your crayons," I turned the sheet over, exposing another faint drawing – this one showed black swirls as thick as smoke in front of a rectangle. The plain circle of the antique doorknob identified the door of room 318, as well as the actual numbers might have.

The third image was a man with x's for eyes surrounded by lightning bolts, no doubt our groundskeeper from the fountain.

"We don't," she admitted, "but it wasn't me, and it wasn't you."

"Well," I flipped another page, "we aren't lacking for creepy on this investigation, are we?"

The next picture was a stick figure portrait of a family, a mom and dad, and two kids standing in front of a ridiculously small house. I'm no art critic, but there's no way even the kids in the drawing could fit through that tiny door.

"Is this a bear?" I asked about the brown mass on the left side of the page.

"I think it's a cow," Meghan offered.

I turned the page to avoid saying something too critical about the artistic license taken.

The fifth image was of a frowning woman in a dark dress with huge, bloody red swirls on the front of it.

"Anne-Marie?" Meghan asked.

"I guess," I looked for more details but couldn't make out

anything useful.

The next picture was of a striped orange cat. I guess they aren't all related to the haunted third floor. It was a cute cat though, certainly the finest one I'd ever seen sketched by a dead kid.

"I want your thoughts on the last picture," she flipped over the cat to reveal the image with the most solid linework so far.

I could see a kitchen on the left side of the drawing with a stove, a sink, and what looked like two refrigerators. The right side had chairs and tables – a lot of them. They were clustered around and stacked from the bottom of the page to the top. That whole area was covered in red, orange, and yellow flames, floor to ceiling.

"It's not a place I've seen in the hotel," I said, though we hadn't wandered around the ground floor and service areas at all.

"I also didn't see any record of a fire like this in my historical research," I couldn't look away from the picture. It was more detailed than the other drawings. I could even make out the pattern on the padded seats of the chairs.

I hadn't seen the chairs, but that pattern matched the carpet I was drinking and critiquing art over.

Meghan finished her drink and left to prepare herself for the evening ahead, whatever that entails for psychics.

We agreed to meet up for a meal before braving 318 again.

Chapter Nineteen

I spent three weeks in Bremen, Germany, once for work. It's a beautiful town with a lot of rules you're expected to observe whether you're a native or not.

My work liaison showed me the sights. The Mercedes factory that used to make U-Boats, the breweries that make decent beer in addition to the swill they sell to American college fraternities. They make no excuses for any of it, and I respect that.

Of course, the Town Musicians of Bremen is a whole, pre-Shrek fairy tale worthy of a whole book and a bunch of assorted musings, but these neglected, geriatric animals, as charismatic as they are, aren't my prominent takeaway from my time in Bremen.

Staying in my hotel next to the airport, I could hop on a train and ride it to old downtown Bremen in just a couple of stops over about ten minutes.

Yes, I met some work colleagues at a brew pub in the historic district, and, double yes, I failed multiple schnapps tests and ended up buying more rounds for the table than I'm comfortable expensing as a line item. But I'd heard a story before I arrived, and I needed to check it out.

Gesche Gottfried was a convicted poisoner and witch in the early 1800s and was publicly executed in the cathedral square on

April 21st, 1831. The site of her execution, the last execution of a witch in Bremen, is marked with a square of black stone among the cobbles.

The locals still hate her for what she did or what she was.

When I finally tracked it down, almost two hundred years later and way too late on a Tuesday night for there to be a lot of people around, there was fresh spit on it.

As a species, we can hold grudges generationally.

What was there to do but face the unknown in room 318?

Admittedly, we had just kind of flailed through previous encounters, but we had more information now. Flailing with purpose just feels different.

I wanted to text a photo of that last Crayola image to Gloria Anderson, but even if the fire wasn't ominous and all over the page, it was a crayon drawing in a childish style, and I couldn't bring myself to explain how we got it. I may see a lot of weird stuff from time to time, but I don't expect anyone to take a colored wax drawing by a dead child at face value.

I would save any faith she still had in our professionalism for when it could do us some good.

Room 318 had several ghosts, but only one who was objectively dangerous. That's not to say any of the countless swirling shadows or even the ghost kids in the hall couldn't cause harm. We just hadn't seen it.

Realistically, when one is dealing with the restless dead, some wiggle room has to be accepted.

I have been in a lot of haunted houses, and I've seen a lot of ghostly activity, but we all have.

It's just that most of that activity is harmless and so unobtrusive that we don't even notice it if we aren't looking for it.

Misplaced keys and dead Wi-Fi routers are very easy to explain away and extremely rarely deadly.

They are kind of perfect for paranormal investigation groups or shows on the Discovery Channel. The witnesses experience something, but the proof is as insubstantial as possible.

I've had cameras and voice recorders die suddenly, and I won't contend that what they edit down from a long slog of an investigation isn't just more compelling.

The big guy in 318 had immediately skipped past the trying-to-get-attention phase and gone right to assault. Meghan mentioned that it still might be acting out as an attempt to communicate, but that hardly mattered to my still-bruised face. And it wouldn't matter to whatever group of untrained Travel Channel fans rent the room next. If I'd had a less thick skull, I wouldn't have survived that first night. Yeah, okay, I hear it now.

I eyed the back wall of the hotel bar and especially the swinging door on the right side where stuffed jalapeño peppers, Buffalo wings, or whatever emerge for the bar, and I suppose where the magic of room service happens. When it opened, I could see a modern kitchen, probably oversized for the hotel on a regular day but perfect for the kind of huge catered events that made the most money for the owners. It was all brushed steel and glaring fluorescent light and just the part I could make out in the narrow view of the doorway could have held four or five people working at once.

The middle of the same wall with the kitchen door was centered with a giant wagon wheel surrounded by a couple of cow skulls and Texas highway signs.

I stood up and walked around the perpendicular wall between the bar and the lobby.

Even with the wagon wheel wall were the lobby restrooms. I had been in the men's room, and it was definitely small, but that's normal when they expect you to rent a room and just pee there.

I walked back towards the kitchen entrance and pushed open the door to get a better look inside.

The far end of the room did have two giant industrial

refrigerators like in the drawing, but they were backed up against a wall that was too close to be opposite the lobby restrooms.

There was space unaccounted for. That is what happens when you refurbish old buildings, trying to make something useful out of old, pointless space. Things don't ever line up quite right.

There is a solid argument that people working on self-improvement have similar issues.

I slipped out onto the patio and climbed over the railing to check out the alley between the Fountain House and the next building.

There was a back entrance for the kitchen and then a single rolling garage door over a short loading dock. It was locked.

I was willing to bet this is where the hotel stores extra furniture for conventions and other events.

Right across the wall from two refrigerators. And every bit as flammable as the rest of the hotel.

I paced it out and figured it could extend as far over as the hotel front desk. They'd probably have a service entrance back there.

I would ask Thad before heading back up to the third floor.

As I turned back up the alley to climb back into the patio, I noticed fresh paint on the wall at the corner of the building.

I pulled out my phone and scrolled through the pictures from the cemetery.

The strange symbols from Bobby Rose's grave had been replicated here at the hotel.

Chapter Twenty

In the interest of avoiding a ton of questions and possible panic, I decided to leave my vest and all my ghost-hunting gear in the car.

Meghan was waiting at the crowded burger place we had settled on. She had traded her normal flowy dress for jeans and a black shirt. Her hair was bound up in a tight braid and there were more crystals than normal hanging around her neck. I guess this was gearing up for hunting bears on the spooky side of the street.

"We need a game plan," I said after we had put in our orders. I find it helpful to order a cheeseburger before confronting an active haunting. It's like a last, greasy bit of happiness before spending quality time with the angry dead.

"I think we should work with the assumption that Bobby Rose is our big, bad blob," Meghan apparently thinks a chicken sandwich and a side salad is the way to prepare for an evening of ghost poking. I guess it takes all kinds.

"You're still on the fence about that, right?" I was trying to arrange a layer of poblano peppers across the melted cheddar without completely destroying the structural integrity of my burger, with minimal success.

"I think you're just sympathetic to the mobster for some

reason," she answered.

"Oh, come on," I argued, "His woman done him wrong! Maybe not in the way he thought she did, but he shot her and got killed in prison, so it's still the ingredients for a great folk song!"

"We have enough folk songs," she said, obviously being incorrect, but I would just let that slide. No sense in arguing with the chicken sandwich lady.

"Another complication," I continued, "is that I found similar tagging on the building to what I took photos of at Bobby's grave."

"The next two nights, we have a full moon, too," she looked concerned.

"I assume you don't mean we can open the drapes in 318 and still see pretty well with the lights off."

She shook her head, "It means every wannabe witch in the hemisphere is going to be pitching their spells and expecting a boost from the full moon." She met my blossoming, incredulous look with her own sober gaze, "You don't have to believe it, Lair. They do. If something is happening, it is happening this weekend. I would put money on it."

"Is someone going to be in that alley with the graffiti tonight, or is it going to happen grave side?" Have motion detectors, will travel – that's me.

I could tell she was trying to decide whether I was making fun of her or humoring her or if I honestly was asking for her expert opinion.

She opted to play it straight, which I appreciated, "My best guess is it will be at the hotel, probably where you found the Ogham on the wall."

"I'll set up cameras," I replied instantly, "we will know when they show up."

"Great," she said, "if they are stirring up some activity, we will need to stop them too."

"We can throw it on the pile." Of course I wanted to investigate the whole modern witch angle, but I was committed to establishing the safety of this hotel room for future occupants.

I could be home right now.

The part of my week I was getting paid for had been over for hours, and by any reasonable standard of activity, I should be on my couch with a paperback and under a cat. There was almost nothing in the world I wanted so much.

But I finished my burger and returned to my car.

I planted cameras on the alley dumpsters and on the iron fence around the patio pointed away from the street.

Fine. I could monitor the living. Recording the dead had

been almost pointless to date. I set it to record back to the DVR in my room and to alert my phone when motion was detected since I would be three floors away most of the night.

The bar patio of the hotel was crowded as I installed the cameras, but no one said a word as I zip-tied them into place. I guess that's the advantage of proper costuming again.

If you dress like you belong, people assume you do. The other possibility is that everyone I saw had their full adult disbelief filters in place. Anything that had to do with the supernatural could just be dismissed as nonsense if it isn't a blatant, direct threat to your survival.

I envy it a little, that obliviousness.

I could remember what it was like. Before I had been exposed to the paranormal.

Back when I could believe ghost stories were just fun things that we tell each other in the dark.

Chapter Twenty-One

Meghan and I stood in the third-floor hallway outside of room 318.

I still didn't feel like we had a solid plan, but maybe it was enough to have an objective.

You know how a yawn sets off sympathetic yawns around you? I mean, the mechanism is a sudden intake of oxygen to prime the body for sudden intense activity or violence, so evolution has primed us to consider an observed yawn as a call to action.

My subconscious self-pat-down checking body cam, digital voice recorder, EMF detector, laser thermometer, a baggie of mugwort, and brass bell set off Meghan's own check of whatever she had in her pockets.

"If you need salt, "I offered, "I've got a giant bin of it next door."

"How giant?"

"Twenty-five pounds." I hadn't wanted us to run out, "De-icing salt is surprisingly cheap in central Texas. The tub said it's 'pet safe,' whatever that means when it comes to salt."

She looked at me. "That's a lot of salt."

"Yeah," I admitted, "it's probably enough salt."

"Are we stalling?" she asked.

"I don't know what you're doing," I put the key in the lock, "but I know I am one hundred percent stalling."

I turned the key and pushed open the door.

Hot, muggy air blew past us from the room, scented like old newsprint and hot copper. The room was dark, so I stepped inside and slapped around the wall for the light switch.

The lamp on the nightstand flickered to life, casting the room into harsh shadows.

I stepped further inside and switched on the light in the little bathroom.

Everything looked untouched, exactly as it had been on my very first visit.

The heavy ashtray still rested on the nightstand. I checked for it the way our ancient ancestors probably checked the trees for sabertoothed tigers. Our instincts to mark threats are hard coded and as deep as marrow.

Meghan crawled onto the bed closest to the window and spread out a thick cloth mat in front of her. It was covered in numbers and letters in an intricate, embroidered spiral.

I raised an eyebrow involuntarily.

"Relax," she assured me, "it's not the only tool in my kit, but it's simple and reliable and a good place to start."

"You're going to upset the ladies at Sunday potluck," I warned.

"Spirit boards got a bad rap after *The Exorcist*," she was laying out various rocks and bowls of powdered herbs or incense, "Before that movie spoiled the fun, these things were everywhere. They used to outsell Monopoly."

I switched on my digital voice recorder and slipped it into my shirt pocket, "I'm not here to judge your methods," I told her, "And you'll never catch me at a church potluck anyway."

I paced around the room with my EMF detector, looking for stray electrical currents. The LEDs stayed dark.

Meghan lit a single white candle and a round charcoal puck. As the coal started to turn orange, she began spooning incense on to it and other things from the metal bowls scattered around her. The smoke rose in thick, sweet spirals over her head. I imagined the tiny flame and the lazy smoke raised the already uncomfortable temperature in the room, but logically, I knew that was impossible.

I checked that my flashlight was still clipped to my vest and switched off the lights in the room.

Meghan fished a small metal hoop out of a pocket and set it

on the mat, resting her fingers lightly on the edge of the hoop and allowing her eyes to drift closed.

"Are there any spirits in the room with us?" she asked.

"No," I glanced down at the EMF detector. It was still dark, "I've got nothing."

She turned her head towards me but didn't open her eyes, "I wasn't talking to you, genius."

I wasn't at all embarrassed and it's not like you could see me blush by the light of a single candle across the room anyway.

That single candle took that opportunity to flicker suddenly as if someone had opened a door.

The small hoop began to circle under Meghan's hand as my EMF detector flared to life and jumped into the red, now the brightest light source in the room.

She looked down and read the answer to her question aloud for my benefit, "Yes."

"Who is it?" I asked Meghan, but the metal hoop began to spiral around again in answer.

"Bob," she read.

"Bobby!" I called into the darkness, "We need to talk, Bobby!"

The hoop traced lazy circles across the mat.

Meghan looked up and addressed the room, "Bobby, you've been hurting people, and you need to stop."

The hoop began to move erratically, zigging and zagging across the letters on the mat. In the darkness, I could have sworn it moved faster than Meghan's hands at times, and she seemed to struggle to catch it with her fingers like an errant playing card from a drunken, one-handed shuffle.

"Something is wrong," she shook her head, "The energy is different."

My EMF detector flashed from red to dark several times before giving up and shutting off for good.

"Slow down, Bobby," I tried, "We want to help." I glanced a little anxiously towards the ashtray again. I may be a slow learner, but I'm hardly an idiot.

Meghan looked puzzled, "It's switching back and forth between two symbols and ignoring the letters for now."

"Symbols for what?" The board looked nothing at all like the one Parker Brothers used to crank out, so I was lost.

"Blackthorn and ivy," she said, clarifying nothing.

I leaned over and studied the two symbols from the bouncing hoop and the ones arranged around them. They looked a lot like the ones scrawled on Bobby's gravestone and on the wall out back, all arranged in a ring outside the standard alphabet, numbers and yes/no, and goodbye.

"What's that about?" I asked, pointing at the runic-looking characters.

Meghan waved me down, "I brought it for the letters, but I was hedging our bets with the Ogham script. I didn't expect it to pay off."

Just then, my phone barked an alert at me.

Someone was moving near the Celtic writing in the alley.

Chapter Twenty-Two

With a glance at me, Meghan blew out the candle and scooped up the incense to set it on the bathroom counter while I rushed to the door and held it open.

We sped down the hall and made all kinds of noise thundering down to the ground floor, blasting open the stairwell door and sprinting out to the patio and over the railing – a move which I was already familiar with, but which still drew an angry complaint from my leg, however justified.

Two hoodie-clad figures huddled by the wall near the dumpster, which partially obscured the Ogham script on the wall.

What do you say in a situation like that? I mean, we've got paranormal activity ranging way past the mean (and I've got the facial bruise to prove it), and our only tie to this entire accusation is a half-viewed cemetery sighting, so there isn't a ton of common ground to lean on for a casual greeting.

"What the fuck are you doing?" Seemed apropos, so I went with that.

Once, about a week after I'd adopted Aengus, but before I'd named him, I caught him chewing on the power cable for my DVD player as though it was some nefarious serpent which merited destruction and wouldn't absolutely murder him through his teeth

Ben Franklin style.

So, I had used the exact same phrase and tone.

The reaction was instantaneous.

Both of our late-night visitors tried to stand up and turn, but only one was successful. The other never quite got the balance necessary and fell straight back to the alley pavement with a grunt pitched high enough for me to identify her as female, even before she clawed down her hood and glared at me.

Her friend took off down the alley at a dead run and quickly exited onto the street. Not that I could have caught them at my most aggressive current hobble.

Meghan had already approached the young woman on the ground and was offering her a hand up.

"We don't care about the graffiti or anything," I tried to smile apologetically, "We just need to know what's going on here, and you seem to know something we don't. We're investigating a possible haunting in room 318."

She stood and looked at me warily through heavily shadowed eyes as Meghan clapped another hand over hers in reassurance.

"Really," she smiled a lot more warmly than I had, "come inside and let's have a drink, and you can tell us everything."

"You don't know about Anne-Marie?" she sounded almost incredulous.

"We can compare notes," Meghan kept smiling. I didn't know where she got the energy.

"Either we're working against each other or doubling our efforts for no reason," my face was starting to hurt from trying to look friendly, "We could clear this up with a conversation."

She nodded quickly and shouldered past me for the patio, "We've been interrupted tonight, anyway," she muttered, "I may as well get out of the alley."

"Call your friend and let them know you aren't hurt or arrested," I said to her back. We didn't need the police to show up because her friend made a panicked call to them.

Having tried to explain a paranormal investigation to law enforcement multiple times in the past, I am well aware my tendencies towards snark and issues with authority in general promise the waste of a few hours at least before I'm eventually left alone as a harmless kook. Worst case, it's a night in jail and no charges filed. Some small towns are worse than others.

I will never forgive you, Blue Ridge, Alabama. You know what you did.

Chapter Twenty-Three

Adrenaline is great and all, but I didn't realize how much I was relying on it until it finally burned away as I sat across from our mysterious vandal.

Familiar aches returned with new friends. I had apparently banged my elbow into something, and the opposite ankle was complaining – probably about how much I was relying on it with my other side all messed up with earlier injuries.

I would apologize to my body with the sincerity of whiskey immediately.

"So," I began smoothly, "I'm Lawrence, and this is Meghan, and we're investigating room 318, as I said. How do you figure into this?"

"She's a witch," Meghan said, staring at her, "I don't know why she's involved, but I know that much."

I looked between them. They were locked into some kind of mutual wary glare.

"Okay," if I wanted answers, I would apparently be asking all the questions, "so you're a Wiccan, right?"

Both women turned their gazes on me and said, in eerie parallel, "That's not the same thing."

"See? I'm learning something already," this was getting creepy. I mean, sure, it started creepy, so I guess it's fair to say it was getting creepier. And more complicated. And our time on the clock was as merciless as ever.

I was half expecting some kind of magical duel to play out, but I could only picture it as a LARP with plastic, battery-powered wands – Preferably numbered officially licensed replicas.

I do have my standards.

"How about we start with your name, and then you can tell me how ancient runes on a gravestone and an alley wall play into this?" If I had to keep this stupid smile on my face for much longer, it would be going on the injured reserve list with much of the rest of me.

"I'm Lydia," she sipped at a cup of hot tea, "and they aren't runes. It's just an old alphabet."

"Thanks for the correction," I didn't care.

"Kind of like how runes are an alphabet, but not all alphabets are runes," Meghan helped with the explanation.

"And," Lydia added, "how not all witches are Wiccan, but some Wiccans call themselves witches."

"Got it," I nodded in understanding, "All thumbs are fingers, but not all fingers are thumbs. What's up with the writing, Lydia?"

"It's for Anne-Marie," she said conspiratorially, "you have to know she got murdered unjustly."

"How does defacing the grave of Bobby Rose do anything for Anne-Marie?" And to be fair, at this point I really was committed to understanding the motivations at play here. I mean, it couldn't hurt. Right?

"Someone in my . . . My group . . . had a vision that showed her a spirit trapped here. In Room 318." She looked at us expectantly.

Meghan tracked her meaning faster than I did. Remember, head injury here.

"You can just say 'coven,' Lydia," I rolled my eyes, "We are all adults here."

"You think Bobby is holding her spirit in room 318," Meghan pushed past my remark.

"It's the only thing that makes sense," Lydia grew more emphatic, "you know it's haunted, and everyone knows why."

"And after almost a hundred years," I pieced it together, "almost anyone would start to feel their sanity start to fray."

"She's getting violent," Lydia pleaded, "she's getting violent because she's hurting."

"Fine," Meghan interjected, "explain your spell work on the

tombstone.”

I expected some variation on “a magician never explains her tricks” and was pleasantly surprised when Lydia produced a pen and began to scratch away on a hotel bar napkin.

“This is the symbol for The Morrigan,” she pointed, “she’s a Celtic defender of women.”

She looked up at Meghan, who nodded slightly in return.

Lydia went back to drawing, “And this one means ‘stay true’ because we know Bobby was an asshole, but also whatever Anne-Marie chose to do about it, it didn’t merit her murder.”

“Sure,” I agreed, “What now?”

Meghan answered first, “Lydia and her friend give us until Monday to put this all to rest.”

“Wait,” I broke up the negotiations, “Who is your friend who took off, and exactly how many of you are there?” I wanted to know if Lydia could deliver on this agreement or if she would end up getting voted down, coven-side.

“It was just me and Charlotte in the alley,” she admitted, “She and I are the main members of our collective,” she paused to see if I’d object, “There are about twenty other women who come in and out, but they mostly show up for Wheel of the Year events and our candle making workshops.”

"Like Christmas candles?" I asked, "Snickerdoodle? Peppermint Mocha?"

I got a mighty side-eye in return, "Bayberry is that Christmas scent. It is a money-drawing herb; the cinnamon in Snickerdoodle is a hastening element for spell work. Peppermint is for cleansing and consecration." She smiled at me, not showing teeth but obviously wanting to. "Your 'Christmas' candles were ours before they were stolen by your kind."

"Hey," I argued, "Don't come after me. I'm Jewish. We love candles. Any and all candles. Sometimes, I'll just light a candle because the light is nice or I'm slightly cold."

Meghan stepped back in, "So this working at the graveyard and out back here, that's just you and Charlotte? The rest of the coven wasn't involved?"

"They made some of the candles we used," Lydia said, "the crystals were charged by the group last month."

"That's it?"

"We make the paint together, chalk powder, rosemary, chamomile, and whiskey. It's environmentally friendly and about as traditional as we can get."

I reflexively cupped my hands around my own glass, protectively.

"We make it by the gallon every full moon. It's a kind of spell, too," she finished.

"If you'd said you used Lone Star beer, that would have been the most Austin thing I'd heard since I got here."

"So," Meghan asked, "Will you give us until Monday to make sure Anne-Marie is at rest? We will be as respectful in our process as possible."

Her eyes darted back and forth between us, but she nodded in agreement. "You will let me know that it is done, and she is at rest Monday? If I don't hear from you, we're coming back to help her."

She wrote a phone number on the same napkin as her runes. Or sigils. Or letters or whatever. She slid the napkin over to Meghan.

"I promise," Meghan answered.

Lydia nodded once again and stood up, her phone buzzing from her pocket, "My friend is here. She is my ride."

"Great," I stood and extended my hand, "enjoy the rest of your weekend, Lydia."

With a quick grasp and release, Lydia turned for the lobby and the front exit.

"Well?" I asked Meghan, waving simultaneously for another round and sitting back down.

Meghan slowly nodded as if considering something. "She's full of shit, Lair."

Chapter Twenty-Four

"Look," she started to explain, "She wasn't exactly lying, but what she and her friends are doing is ill-informed at best."

"It sounded pretty harmless," I was out of my depth, but it sounded like witchcraft on the Hallmark Channel to me.

"Oh, I see how it sounds like that," she agreed, "but 'stay true' is a binding as well as an affirmation. Potentially, with a whole coven of intent behind it, it could bottle a spirit up and set it on its original motivation."

"The downfall of Bobby Rose," I offered.

"At the least," she nodded, "but it gets worse."

"Of course it does," I once again wished for a sweltering attic full of harmless murdered children.

She pursed her lips at my fresh glass of whiskey, "I guess we have time for a brief mythology lesson."

"Sláinte," I tipped my glass to her.

"Appropriate," she sighed, "Lydia invoked The Morrigan, and, while she was technically correct, the ramifications were incomplete."

"Look," I wasn't ready to lean into mysticism on account of I'm a slow learner, I guess, "please don't tell me an ancient pagan

Celtic goddess is involved in our hotel haunting in Texas because there frankly isn't enough whiskey in the world to make that make sense for me."

"Again," she set down her drink, "you've got a whole coven believing they are invoking The Morrigan for one facet of her personality. It doesn't need to make sense to you because it makes sense to them, and their belief, however one-dimensional, can play havoc with our would-be simple haunting."

"Would," I took a medium-sized mouthful of my drink and waved for another, "Be."

Meghan bravely muscled forward, "Yes, she is a defender of women, but she also has other aspects,

"She is a warrior, a nature goddess, a druid," she paused, "She's a psychopomp and the Chooser of the Slain."

Again, I could hear the capital letters. I really needed to learn how to do that, if only to reinforce a strong Password Policy when I'm at work.

"The Morrigan," she continued, "can not only usher a spirit between the physical realm and the other world, but she also decides who lives and who dies in a battle to the death."

"The holy coin toss?" I asked.

"No," Meghan answered, "it costs her every time, but she

does it because that's her job."

I needed to hit Wikipedia, obviously, but it could wait. We had active ghosts in room 318 and Meghan and I were the only things between them and a bunch of rookies becoming paranormal Lunchables.

"It ties into what the spirit in the room said," she explained, "the ivy grows freely, but it parasitizes whatever it grows on. Ancient people considered it able to wander between this world and the next."

"That sounds related," I admitted.

"And the blackthorn is authority and control, triumph over adversity, and hardiness over death," she finished.

"So, we've got an angry spirit," I started to put it together, "who has power over other spirits and controls their ability to cross over."

"No, it's worse," Meghan shook her head sadly, "she controls them completely."

"Alright," I took another long drink, "Let's say this is all true. I'm honestly a little out of my element, but fine. How does it change what we do?"

Meghan considered for a moment, "We still have at least one angry, violent ghost in 318, and if this coven has been successful, this ghost has a hell of a lot more power than it did before they started messing with it."

"The paint outside wasn't more than a week old, so there's a chance the experiences in room 318 would have been far milder than after it got painted when we showed up."

"And if Anne-Marie really is juiced up," Meghan added, "and controlling the other ghosts in the hotel, then we have to disrupt that before we set about putting her to rest."

"What do we do about this death goddess?' I planned to just add whatever she said to my mental to-do list.

"The Morrigan isn't a death goddess," she corrected me, seeming to subconsciously slip into lecture mode, "not like Anubis or Arawn, or Hel or Pluto. Irish myth doesn't pigeonhole like that. And I don't know what we do. If anything."

Not for the first time, I wondered what Meghan's day job was.

"Maybe I can clean up the wall tomorrow, and we can try again?"

"Yeah," she pondered, "maybe. I think we need to go back in tonight. Maybe we can get something else, but I have to make sure the space is clean for tomorrow either way."

"So," I smiled in a way I knew was obnoxious, "we think

maybe Bobby isn't the bad guy here, right?"

"He's *a* bad guy," Meghan defended, "but possibly not *the* bad guy."

"He's not leveraging an Irish deity to make ghost children miserable and torment a groundskeeper," I clarified, "but he's still possibly a jerk."

"Probably," she smiled, "he's probably a jerk."

"Yeah," I said wistfully, "he just gets me."

Chapter Twenty-Five

We returned to room 318, not exactly confident but with the distinct swagger of being better informed.

No one had any illusions that we couldn't be surprised, and the stakes were more mystical and intangible, but we knew what we faced. So, we faced it together.

I opened the door to room 318 and stepped in with authority and purpose I didn't necessarily feel but needed to project.

The room was still hot and muggy, like a dingy carpeted swamp.

It smelled of charcoal and grave dirt and dry, cracked bones.

This, with an almost imperceptible smoky line of incense still hanging in the air at shoulder height.

Meghan moved swiftly, checking the incense burner in the bathroom but leaving it in place and then grabbing bowls and ceremonial stuff I couldn't catalog and sorting them into a pouch over her shoulder.

I abhor silence, so I decided to play diplomat, "Anne-Marie," I said pleasantly, "I'm going to ask you politely to release the spirits in this room."

An icy breeze whispered across the back of my neck, making

me flinch involuntarily.

"Ugh," I groaned, "I'm going to take that as a no."

The temperature dropped precipitously, and the lights began to slowly flicker.

Dark, shadowy shapes again began to flow about the room as a too familiar large form began to fill the far corner.

"Shit," I complained, "I was just asking!"

"The children!" Meghan reeled, "the children are all around us!"

I had no idea how she could identify the faceless shapes around us as anything but "bad," but I wasn't about to argue with her.

"Are we staying, or are we going?" I slowly turned, keeping an eye on the large shape, which was even then forming legs and arms and easing towards us.

"I'm going to talk to the children," she said, kneeling on the floor and closing her eyes.

I saw her eyebrows move animatedly in the flickering light and tried to track the insubstantial progress of the big apparition as it shambled across the carpet towards her back.

She didn't speak, at least not out loud, but the dark swirling shapes began to slow and drift downward.

The temperature dropped further. I heard ice forming inside the glass of the window. And the whispers.

I could hear the whispers again.

I shivered, but I couldn't blame it solely on the cold.

There was a stereo click as the bedside lamp and bathroom light both went dark.

I slapped at my vest, and after what felt like an eternity in the whispering darkness, my hand closed on the little flashlight.

Not wanting to interrupt whatever Meghan had going on, I settled for raising the flashlight to my ear and keeping my thumb on the button, ready to flood the room with light.

A deliberate flutter of black feathers brushed the back of my hand. How could I tell they were black in the pitch darkness of the hotel room from hell?

They *felt* black.

I shuddered and almost pressed the button for light in cold desperation.

"Meghan?" I called into the room, "we need to wrap this up!"

With my free hand, I again flailed around my suddenly too

many supposed-to-be-handy pockets and drew out something I was almost certain would be useless.

Both hands occupied, I stood in the dark and stared hard at where I'd last seen Meghan kneeling. By memory, I shuffled myself blindly between her back and the hulking, shadowed thing that had been heaving itself silently toward her.

Chivalry may not be dead, but it was about to need fresh underwear.

Meghan collapsed backward, falling against the backs of my legs.

I stepped forward by reflex into a wall of bitter, aching cold.

Muscles locked, and something took a highlighter to my accumulation of injuries. My battered leg gave out first, and I struggled to not fall on top of Meghan.

I was mostly successful.

From the floor, I triggered the flashlight in my right hand and clicked again to set off the strobe light.

The dark shape reached down for me, and I frantically shook the brass bell in my left hand.

Metallic notes rang out in the room, concentric circles of sound that hit the shapes around us with a physical force, dissipating the entities enough for me to struggle to my feet again and drag

Meghan's unconscious form for the door again.

The strobing flashlight gave up just as I got the hotel room door open, and I pulled Meghan the rest of the way outside.

Chest heaving, I leaned against the wall of the hallway and looked down at the tiny brass bell in my hand.

I should have bought one of these years ago.

I propped open the door to my room and carried Meghan inside. Figuring she would be unconscious for a few hours, I set her down on the bed by the window and laid down on the other bed to rest my eyes for a moment.

I'm once again on a quiet cul-de-sac, looking at the front of a comfortably worn house. Walking up the front steps, I can't help but look up at the beadboard ceiling over the small front porch. It's covered in spiderwebs and abandoned wasp nests.

It's haint blue.

As I push inside, I note, detached, that the home is empty. The family that lived there has left, and as the sole remaining human occupant, I head directly to the desk in the living room to pour a drink from the bottle sitting there.

There's no need for ice – that would just delay the effect.

Strange shapes cavort in the reflection of the plate glass window in front of me. Humanoid, but only vaguely. Reptilian or insectoid, bulbous or lumpy, they range in size from eighteen inches to well over seven feet tall, looming over me in mute menace.

I close the blinds, ending the reflection to sit alone in the dark with my drink.

It is foolish for any of us to assume we are ever really alone in the dark.

Chapter Twenty-Six

One Friday night years ago, I took in a local play at the Henderson County Performing Arts Center in Athens, TX. As much as I do, unironically, love community theatre, I really wanted access to the parking lot.

The east side of that parking lot butts up against Fuller Park, which isn't really an actual park, but more a densely wooded area situated at a corner of two rural roads. The play let out after dark, so I was not disturbed as I walked past my car and into the dense undergrowth and thick shadows of the ancient trees of this long-abandoned space.

I was investigating solo, but even if I'd had a partner or a group to work with, I wouldn't have invited anyone. The story was just too bizarre.

According to local legend, a circus train derailed in Athens, Texas, in or around 1930, killing a bunch of various animals and clowns and what not and releasing a bunch of monkeys into the woods around the crash site. I told you it was weird.

Of course ghost monkeys haunt this patch of forest. That's just science, right?

But a local preacher bought the land and captured the surviving monkeys and just kind of kept them.

When his wife died in 1933, he buried her in what is now known as Fuller Park, adjacent to the now-vacant monkey cages that still exist there. There are also random sheds and outbuildings and an old tow truck with four flat, dry-rotted tires.

Why Reverend Fuller kept the monkeys is up for debate.

Some people say he used them in dark occult rituals, and some say he did strange, unscientific medical experiments on them out in the woods.

It's possible the guy just liked monkeys, and that's completely okay, in my opinion.

Well, I mean, for the 1930's, anyway. It was a different time, and those monkeys were just loose in the east Texas woods, so it wasn't like they'd survive a winter without shelter. Or maybe they would. I'm not a primatologist. I barely understand how people work.

I saw the monkey cages with their iron bars and tin roofs, and I saw the three graves of Fuller Park, the Reverend and his wife and their only child (who is only marked with a bench, so I couldn't tell you if it was a son or a daughter) and the woods filled with empty beer cans and bottles and scrawled with occult graffiti.

And, at times, I heard the chitters and howls of primates in the trees around me, invisible in the dark forest.

The electric lamp I'd clipped to my belt barely cut into the foggy night around me, so I was constantly banging my shins and knees against fallen logs and exposed roots, and more than once, I pitched over into the damp soil of Fuller Park.

Feeling a persistent itching, I pulled up my pants leg to find ticks attached to my skin, so thick against each other that they looked like the scales on a snake, vaguely writhing against each other, ankle to kneecap.

By the time I got back to my car and checked again in the parking lot lights, there was no sign of them.

Saturday morning seemed to arrive brutally early, but by the time the sun rose enough to start to really bake the Austin pavement, Meghan and I had regrouped at Magnolia Café for brunch. I know. I have a process.

Wraparound windows let in plenty of light with the main dining area surrounding a U-shaped, old-school counter for anyone nostalgic for circular spinning seats and no lumbar support.

There was just enough chrome to make the place feel authentic, though the split vinyl booth seats patched with duct tape personally spoke to me of the pedigree of this regional staple of a diner with ultimate authority.

The sound of a popping griddle and the smell of cooking meat did as much to wash away the feeling of dread from the night before as the sunlight itself did.

Though I'd never file an expense report, for the record, I had the queso omelette and coffee from a battered stainless-steel carafe left on the table while Meghan had gingerbread pancakes and Irish breakfast tea.

I may not have understood her methods, but the lady knew her way around brunch, and I cannot overstate the respect that earns from me.

"Okay," I said, blowing steam across a cup of too-hot coffee I fully intended to burn my mouth to consume anyway, "What do we have now that we didn't before our visit last night?"

"Besides a headache?" Meghan asked.

"Oh," I covered my face in shock, "Your headache is new? How adorable!"

She threw a slice of banana at me.

"How about we pick off her support staff?" I ventured, "You said the swirling shadows and the children in the hallway are the same guys?"

"They have the same energy," she started, "I got a solid feel for the vibration during the bedtime story."

"Is there a way to," I struggled, "neutralize, I guess, the dead kids?" God, this was weird. If I didn't have my own nightmares in hot rotation, I'd be accumulating fresh ones for sure.

"Yeah," she scooped some whipped cream with a wad of pancake, "I think I can mitigate that this evening. I have a plan."

"So, I can leave the hallway of restless dead urchins to you?" I had my own preparations to make, but I was more than happy to outsource the ghostly children.

"It's not something I've tried, but yes."

"Fair enough," I poured more coffee into my still-warm mug and added half-and-half and artificial sweetener in part because I was used to it but mostly because I had a rough admission to get through, "Because I don't know if you've noticed, but I'm not operating at a hundred percent right now."

"You mean how you're all beat to hell and also all old and used up?" Her mocking eyebrows feigned innocence.

Beau Neumann slid into the booth next to her with a Styrofoam container.

"How are my favorite ghost hunters this morning?" he beamed at us both through an ingenious neck swivel.

"Hey, Beau," Meghan smiled at him, "we're so glad you could join us!"

"What have you learned?" He leaned in, eyebrows wriggling like he was expecting the best high society gossip of the season.

"Anne-Marie is certainly active," I allowed, "but Austin has a local coven whacking her hornet's nest."

"Which coven?" He leaned forward eagerly.

I don't know why I'd thought the existence of a coven of witches in Austin would be scandalous to Beau, but obviously, I had been stupid to make assumptions in a town that was so proudly weird.

"There's more than one?!"

Beau and Meghan both looked at me like I'd wandered in from the pasture following my long-horned mother that morning.

"There is a traditional coven that operates out of the historic district," Beau started, opening his Styrofoam clamshell to reveal a mountain of eggs and cheese and meat, which he began to liberally spoon salsa over, "a group of kitchen witches that are delightful company, but rumor is they only joined a group for a discount at Williams Sonoma. . ."

Meghan picked it up, "The University has three separate occult student groups, and I think at least two are technically covens. There's a traditional Celtic coven, which is a branch of a larger Appalachian original coven dating back to the 1600s, and, finally, a local bookstore hosts weekly magic classes, but they spell it with a 'k.'"

"Spell it with a 'k' all you want. Magic is still bullshit with a K, alright?" I defended.

"How does it feel to be the normal one, Lawrence Miller, ghost hunter?" Meghan asked.

"I'm not a fan," I replied.

"Admit it," she chuckled, "you're a Muggle."

"Hey," I defended, "we can call ourselves that. You don't get to call us that."

We continued to discuss ghosts in general and the ins and outs of central Texas polite society.

When I opened my wallet to eventually pay our tab, nestled among my ID and credit cards and an assortment of paper money was a single, four-inch-long, glossy black feather.

Chapter Twenty-Seven

We split up after our chat at the diner and I headed back to the Cauldron.

Meghan had given me a weird shopping list for the "authentic" Dry Goods and Sundries shop tucked into a little tourist-friendly corner off the state capitol grounds, but I wanted to get my witchy research out of the way first.

I stepped into the little bookstore and was once again blanketed in a haze of incense smoke and scented candle soot.

Was there an Idiot's Guide to Witchcraft? Maybe there was a Magic with a K for Dummies?

Probably not, but I was content to browse the titles anyway.

I had no interest in putting anything into practice, but I wanted to be prepared for what someone who did have that interest could have stirred up in room 318.

I know one card trick, and it is exactly that – a trick. These waters were unfamiliar, and I wasn't swimming so well to begin with.

I walked past a shelf loaded with various stones and crystals. There was a polished clear orb of quartz (or something) on a pedestal in the center with a folded warning sign in "magick" marker next to it with instructions to cover it with a cloth when unattended.

I asked the clerk why, figuring there was supposed to be some chance the Dark Lord would be looking back at you in search of his lost magic ring.

He said, "Because if the sunlight hits it weird, it'll burn your house down."

Fair enough.

There was a sealed glass cabinet full of little statues.

Some I recognized right away. Mary from Nativity scenes made several appearances, and I could tell Mercury by the little wings on his ankles. Bushy-bearded Thor looked like a biker with a hammer. There was a jackal-headed Egyptian guy I vaguely remembered as being about death or judgment. Which reminded me…

"Excuse me," I addressed the fun-killing fire marshal behind the counter, "is one of these The Morrigan?"

"Yeah," he eased back from around the register and produced a key to unlock the cabinet, "actually, a few of them are."

He picked up a single statuette with three figures on it, "You've got your default maiden, mother, and crone aspect, our best seller."

He handed it to me. It looked heavier than it was. It wasn't plastic. Maybe painted resin?

A robed and hooded figure was produced next, "our local Druid community prefers this one."

Austin has a local Druid community? Doesn't that require some kind of bog?

We traded and I looked it over. A delicate ring of braided knot-work encircled the base.

He reached far back into the cabinet and dug out a third figure, a young woman with long black hair and primitive armor. She held a sword upraised in one hand and had great black wings unfurled behind her. A group of ravens clustered around her sandaled feet.

"Chooser of the Slain, right?" I asked.

"Yep," he nodded, "bloodier than eenie, meenie, miney, moe, right? Which is weird because that comes from the Irish words for one, two, three, and four anyway."

I bought it.

And a book on the Celtic "Ghost World".

And a second bell for Meghan. She hadn't seen the last one work, but I wasn't sending her into 318 without a tiny bit of brass insurance.

The Dry Goods and Sundries store had most of the things on Meghan's list, plus a great deal of kitsch. I loaded up.

What I couldn't find there I picked up at Target. Tell the ghosts that is a fancy word for wagon train or something.

I also loaded up on scrubbing sponges, mild abrasive, a couple of bottles of water, some dish soap, and a plastic bucket.

I parked outside the gates of Oakwood cemetery and walked the familiar path back to the Rose family plot in solemn silence and set about scrubbing clean the headstone of Robert "Bobby" Rose.

I had no illusion that this would help with our ongoing issue, but it didn't matter. Bobby, almost inarguably a real bastard, had no one to show up for him and scrub clean his last physical marker.

Sure, it might sever the connection to whatever weird magical working was amping up the activity in room 318, but that wasn't why I was crouched in a cemetery just after noon on a Saturday.

Whatever he had done in life, he wasn't choosing to do harm now. And in my sleep-deprived state, I couldn't begrudge anyone the right to a peaceful rest.

By the time I stood up, the grave marker was once again a brilliant white, free of the markings that had marred its surface and chained a spirit to the single worst day of its short, brutal life.

I'd have left flowers, but I hadn't bought any, and also bringing flowers to an unrelated male friend probably crosses some kind of line, and however enlightened I can claim to be, I'm still beholden to the Bro Code.

"Rest in peace, Bobby," I settled on as an invocation. And I truly hoped he would.

I headed back to my hotel room and fitfully napped away the afternoon.

I'm again on a quiet cul-de-sac, looking at the front of a comfortably worn house. Walking up the front steps, I can't help but look up at the beadboard ceiling over the small front porch. It's covered in spiderwebs and abandoned wasp nests.

It's haint blue. I know it won't help.

I step inside and immediately hear the voices. They aren't shy. They don't hold back. They utter things about every insecurity I have dating back to middle school, voices layering one over another as I stagger through the too-empty house, desperate to get to the part of the day I can numb with alcohol.

I am too slow. I am always too slow.

Chapter Twenty-Eight

Saturday night in Austin kicks off mid-afternoon with a growing crowd increasingly stumbling up and down Sixth Street as the sun slips behind the tall buildings of downtown.

Over the years, the clubs and bars surrounding Sixth have claimed the academic careers of many college students and ended the political aspirations of a shocking number of elected officials.

One weekend years ago, I happened to catch a live performance of a great Scottish band I'd never heard of, and the following month, when I thought about it again, I went to track down an album. I learned the lead singer had drowned a handful of days after I'd seen them play.

They never recorded again.

I don't blame Sixth Street in Austin for that, but I wouldn't be surprised if someone did.

Meghan and I regrouped at the Chupacabra Cantina for fish tacos and salsa served by the half gallon.

We sat, bathed in garish fluorescent lighting, next to a large, glossy, fiberglass statue of a bipedal, wolf-like monster with the horned head of a goat.

The slightly-too-loud music bounced back at us from walls

covered in license plates and liberated traffic signs.

In short, it was perfect.

Meghan had telegraphed her idea to mitigate the ghost children, and I was committed to backing her play. Even though I thought it was insane at my most generous.

"So," I said, absolutely swamping a tortilla chip with verde sauce to the point where the structural integrity would be compromised in seconds. "Kids first, then the big ghosts? Or how do you want to handle this?"

Meghan was working her way circularly around an avocado salad, which sounded entirely inappropriate for confronting dead anything but actually looked pretty decent. If you tell anyone I said that, I'll deny it.

"Any juice we can bleed off of Anne-Marie will help us," she nodded, "and the kids are low-hanging fruit."

"We really need to get some points on the board," I agreed.

"Right now," she explained, "the children are, at sometimes literally, a cloud obscuring whatever the real issues in room 318 are."

"So, we get the kids off the field and then tackle whatever shambles out next?" I don't resolve hauntings. I don't believe it's possible. But I didn't have an alternative. I also don't use sports metaphors and you see how that was going.

When in haunted Rome, right?

"Theory time," I announced, "Who is the big guy?"

"The one we've seen?"

I brushed past the thought of multiple, huge, hulking entities in my memory, "Yeah, the aggressive one."

"It's felt different every time," she pondered, "possibly, it's different spirits. It could also be different emotions, though."

"We have to resolve that," I touched my forehead, "I can't leave before I'm sure no one is getting an ashtray to the face."

"You saw that spirit throw the ashtray?" She asked.

I hadn't.

I hadn't seen anything throw it.

I had just assumed.

"It's just likely," I clarified, "we can figure it isn't the children, and The Hulk is the only other ghost we have seen manifesting."

"It's not the only ghost in 318," Meghan met my eyes, "There are layers of drama and tragedy and bad juju in there."

"Thank you."

She paused to dip into one of the multiple salsas, "Are we really calling the big apparition 'The Hulk'?"

"My EMF detector isn't tuned for Gamma rays," I admitted, "but look at my forehead."

"I see your point," she conceded.

"I'm not used to this type of investigation," I explained, "Normally, I'm sitting in a dark attic or basement for hours with nothing going on, logging hours and hours of audio and video I have to review later to pick out the possible ghosts. And those are for hauntings where people are actually being bothered by activity."

"Room 318 doesn't waste time, does it?"

"It's off any chart I could use to measure it."

"And it's getting worse with every visit," she said, "like it's waiting for us."

"Obviously, burning a little sage and asking the spirit politely to leave is a non-starter," I said, "So what's the plan for the dead adults in the room?"

"My plan," she stressed, "is to do a full spiritual cleansing of the space, but I'm not confident I can get that done tonight."

I gestured with a queso-saddled chip for her to continue.

"Our current theory is that one ghost, probably Anne-Marie,

is controlling the rest of them. When we start messing with her connection to the hallway children, she's going to notice."

"And we hate it when she does that," I agreed.

"So, while I've got a reliable and tranquil purification ritual," she punctuated with a sip of margarita, "smart money is we're going to be improvising early and often."

Oddly, my first feeling was liberation. The important part of having a plan is sticking to it. At work, I like to tell the executives that my process is "organic," which is just business talk for making stuff up on the fly and fixing things as they break.

My second feeling was cold dread because the things that could definitely break were Meghan and me.

Chapter Twenty-Nine

One Sunday night during my senior year in high school, a friend and I decided to drive to Oklahoma. We were sober, or as sober as the brain gets when you're seventeen and emotionally done with school.

We both lived and went to school in north Texas, so getting back in time for class with Monday's Durant Daily Democrat from Durant, Oklahoma, seemed like a really important and reasonable thing to do at the time.

I can still remember the confused look on the clerk's face at the gas station where we bought two copies of the paper, some beef jerky, and Mountain Dew before climbing back into our car and heading back south. That had been our whole chosen mission, and we had completed it.

What was supposed to be a straight shot back to Dallas somehow, through caffeine or exhaustion, veered west at some point, and we ended up passing through Bowie, Texas, and then attempting to angle back towards civilization to the southeast. Getting back home in time to get to Monday morning classes on time was the grown-up and responsible thing to do, and we would not be deterred.

Until on our way into Chico, we saw a sign marking Green

Elm Cemetery Road. The barely dirt trail headed off into a dense thicket. There were no streetlights, no electric lights at all in that direction, honestly.

But we decided, in that impulsive way teenagers do, that there might be a story down Green Elm Cemetery Road, and it might even be more impressive than a fresh copy of the Durant Daily Democrat. As if that is even possible.

At the end of the increasingly overgrown dirt road was a small scattering of tombstones, probably less than 30 in all. While we walked around them, lit up as best we could with carefully angled headlights, we could see most dated from the late 1800s, with a couple from the early 1900s.

The ground occasionally gave way a bit under our careful steps, indicating that there were probably a good many more unmarked graves.

The post oak trees, in the harsh, one-directional light of the headlights, seemed to lean in towards us. The normal sounds of small creatures and night birds were absent.

This wasn't a place for the living anymore. This wasn't a place they frequently visited, if ever, anymore.

When neither of us wanted to be the first to return to the car, we seemed to silently agree we were done with our visit at the same time and began to head back up the dirt path, headlights striking twisted mesquite trees like lightning against the pitch black darkness of the roadside forest.

A left turn instead of the proper right in the darkness ended at an old iron bridge across a branch of the draught-parched Trinity River.

Again, as if by unspoken agreement, we stepped out of the car to investigate.

Iron girders crisscrossed the structure, and ancient, dry-rotted boards stretched across to the other side of the river. It didn't look like it would support a car, and it probably wasn't safe for two stupid kids on foot, but we started walking across it anyway.

At about the halfway point, we could see that there was no road on the other side. So long out of use, it had been completely reclaimed by nature on the other side.

The sound of the river tumbling over stones in the dark was soothing and a light breeze passed over us that had probably been blocked by the dense vegetation around us before. Out over the river, we were exposed.

Which is why the sound of a woman's scream from upriver was so jarring we both clutched the iron railing and looked frantically toward the sound.

We could see a woman with dark hair in a white dress thrashing around and continuing to scream below us. But she wasn't in the water.

She was easily a dozen feet above the current water level of the Trinity, and she passed under the bridge and down the river, still flailing and shrieking and floating in midair as she went out of sight around the curve of the river.

Was she possibly buried in that little cemetery down the road? Had she drowned during some flood years and years ago?

We just knew she wasn't alive and that we couldn't have helped her. And getting closer to her wasn't something either of us had felt like doing.

We went back to the car and drove home and never spoke of our trip to that bridge again.

Graduation happened a few months later, and we found fewer and fewer things to speak about before we both left for separate colleges and never spoke again.

Like I said, teenagers do dumb things.

With a few hours to wait before we started Operation: Dead Kids, I settled into a comfortable chair at the bar at the Fountain House with my laptop in front of me. I had decided that I'd review some of the early footage I'd recorded in room 318. Sure, I could learn something maybe, but I suppose even more I needed to embrace the comfort of my regular process.

This is the boring, routine, everyday kind of ghost hunt I was used to.

I flagged the files for motion and started frame by frame, examining what I had. Gloria would be pleased with a couple of good screenshots for her marketing materials, if nothing else.

I had just dismissed approximately the thousandth orb picture as dust (these old hotel fixtures seem to just bleed the stuff) when I stopped on a still frame showing a glow from the bathroom.

I went to the same time stamp on the camera facing more directly into the room and hit play.

There was a flickering light in there, like the flame of a single candle sitting on the counter.

The bathroom mirror seemed to amplify that light, throwing it back against the wall. I had been in that bathroom a few times and there was never a candle in there.

The light had shuddered against the wall for a few seconds in total.

I went back and played it through again at half speed, leaning towards the screen as if that would help.

At half speed, I caught a glance of movement against the back wall, so I went back again and played it slower.

In the middle point of the clip, there was a vague shadow at quarter speed.

Frame by frame, it revealed itself.

The candle cast a shadow of a tall, angular woman in a long flowing dress painted itself in stark detail across the bathroom wall.

I ordered another drink and continued my review of the video.

There's a weird kind of Zen in reviewing haunting videos after the fact. Like you want to expect some kind of silver bullet, indisputable proof of the supernatural.

But as technology improves, the standard of evidence moves a little faster.

Photoshop came out in 1990, so any photographic evidence since that is suspect. Dismissible even.

At some point, you just have to accept that any measure of proof is subjective. I know what I've seen, and I'll tell the ghost stories I need to tell.

I can't control the beliefs of anyone else.

There was a black mist, like a serpentine shadow, that clung to the ceiling for most of an hour, like it was watching. Or waiting for something.

It gradually resolved itself into a noose hanging in the center of the room. Gently swaying, though I knew there was no breeze.

It faded away. Harmless, I guess, if creepy as all hell.

What I never saw was the Hulk. I don't think I'd expected to, though.

That kind of manifestation seemed to take a while, which meant it had to take considerable effort or energy. There wouldn't be much point in doing it to stomp around an empty room for a while.

The big guy only showed up when something needed doing, like attacking a couple of paranormal nerds.

There were odd shadows and more dust, but eventually, I ran out of time to review any more.

We had an appointment on the third floor to empty out the daycare of the dead.

Chapter Thirty

Meghan set up shop in the third-floor hallway just outside of room 318.

She had arranged a circle of candles on little silver cups on the carpet and the now familiar scent of whatever incense she chose again hovered in visible clouds around her.

An inch-high ring of pet-safe driveway salt encircled her. Score one for bargain shopping.

She sat cross-legged, her hands on her knees, and softly began a chant while I kept an eye on the stairway door, ready to grab her and flee.

I mean strategically withdraw. Whatever.

Shadows began to move through the fixed hallway lighting, spiraling around and eventually settling into their places on the floor in a loose circle around Meghan.

She opened her eyes.

"Hello, children," she smiled, "thank you for joining us."

I sat down against the wall myself, preparing for what was next, and second, third, and fourth thinking about this plan.

Meghan clapped her hands and began to speak, "When I was a kid, I used to live on a street where there was a haunted house.

There was a big, happy family living there. One night, one of the kids was playing with matches, and the youngest boy in the family dropped a match on his bed. He was too scared to get up and call for help, so he just let it burn. His parents and two sisters burned to death in the flames.

"Many years later, at a sleepover, me and my friends decided to scare each other by telling ghost stories. It was getting close to midnight, and since we couldn't scare ourselves, we decided it would be fun if we went to the haunted house at night. We went through the gate together and up to what was left of the door. There was a faint smell of smoke, and small clouds of ash were blowing in the breeze. But then we noticed there was no wind."

As she spoke, the dark shapes gradually became the tiny forms of the children we had seen earlier, all intently focused on Meghan as she continued her story.

"In the ash clouds, figures started to take shape, and gray hands extended from the formations. Screams emerged from the ashes as we turned to flee. They yelled, "Help us, we're burning!" With the idea that we would be safe as soon as we were outside the home, we took off running. But the shouts and shapes of ash followed us. The smell of burning was almost overpowering as we got closer to my house, and when we opened the door, I looked over my shoulder and saw someone reaching out to grab me.

We piled through my front door, slamming it behind us, and ran up the stairs to my room, slamming that door tight, too. None of us expected to sleep, but the fear had exhausted us, and we fell into a deep slumber."

Apart from Meghan's voice, the hallway was as silent as a tomb. No other voice, no traffic or weather sounds, and I was breathing as shallowly as I could, a bit on the edge of my carpeted seat myself.

She shuddered. If it was an act, it was a convincing one.

"The next morning over breakfast, we felt better," she continued, "eventually even laughing about it and deciding it had all been in our imaginations."

"Brunch is better," I breathed.

Meghan glared at me but pressed on, "We decided to head back to the haunted house in the sunlight to prove we were unafraid. Opening the front door of my house, we were hit with the smell of burning paint, the light blue of the door having been marred with burned handprints, two sets at the top, a lower two sets of smaller prints, and, at the bottom, a single set of the smallest handprints."

This wasn't a story that would be helping me sleep, but that wasn't the point, I guess.

"Lair," she addressed me, "Please give the children their

good night gifts."

I opened the made-in-China burlap sack printed with "Texas Pecans" I'd bought at the souvenir store and began to produce toys, scattering them across the carpet.

I'd bought bags of marbles, sets of jacks, several rag dolls, a variety of rubber balls, and four copies of "The Littlest Cowpoke" picture book.

I set the toys out around me and breathlessly waited.

The air in the hallway seemed to slowly solidify like one of those awful salads from the seventies, except it wasn't gelling around olives and canned tuna. It was firming up around us.

The shadowy forms around us began to solidify as well into the shapes of the hallway children, details slowly painting themselves across the little, huddled figures.

They clustered around me, inspecting the little piles of toys spread out around us.

A little girl in an age-faded gingham dress boldly grabbed at one of the books and stepped back with it quickly, pressing herself against the wall.

A little boy in what looked like a soot-stained nightshirt darted in and grabbed a rubber bouncing ball, the largest.

He also rapidly retreated to the wall next to the door, and it seemed like a system had been created.

One by one, the other ghostly children stepped forward, grabbed a toy, and lined up against the far wall, examining their new possessions and watching their fellow kids select their own prizes.

Meghan had returned, eyes closed, to chanting during this process, her voice pitched low and the rhythm almost hypnotic.

I briefly wished she'd seen this, then remembered I had another step to complete.

I shook open a bag of penny candy from the tourist trap of a general store (and which also came out to about seven cents apiece due to inflation, I'd done the math while grumbling over the price of progress before paying wirelessly with my phone) and offered a handful to the line of spectral children stretching down the hallway.

"Alright, kids," I didn't feel up to smiling reassuringly, so I didn't try, "we got you candy, too. Take a piece and go to sleep."

The little boy with the largest rubber ball stepped up and reached out for my hand, which I quickly closed into a fist.

"Listen to Miss Meghan, okay?" I slowly opened my hand again, "we think you need to sleep for a few days at least. Okay?"

Black eyes met my own and my spine complained about the cold.

But the boy nodded, grabbed a butterscotch, and faded back

into the wall, candy and ball and everything.

"Neat trick," I observed.

One after another, each ghostly child selected a piece of candy and passed into the wall until Meghan and I were alone again in the hallway.

"Are they gone for good?" I asked.

"Eh," Meghan sounded exhausted, and our night was just starting, "the term 'for good' is pretty useless in this context, but the kids all took their gifts to the Ghost World, which takes a lot of energy."

She verbally capitalized again. Damn it.

How did she do that? Sure, I'd seen her summon and dismiss spirits and bribe child ghosts into getting out of the way of the grownups and communicating with the dead. But her verbal sorcery was impressive.

I made another mental note to ask about it after we wrestled room 318 into submission.

Room 318 which was now making horrible noises from behind the locked door with its antique doorknob.

Chapter Thirty-One

Meghan nodded at me with a sideways look, and I smirked as I unlocked the door.

In for a penny, in for a . . . quid, I guess? They're back on the pound sterling since Brexit but I've never heard someone from England call it that.

I was, again, stalling.

Not unreasonably.

I gusted breath out of pursed lips and shoved open the door. You want to start some shit in our physical realm, you'd better expect some smartassed pushback from me. To be fair, it was my only weapon.

A handful of herbs and an unreasonable amount of driveway salt seemed to not count, really.

A sickly, pained wail sounded from the dark interior of the room. It wasn't exactly human, but it pulled on the part of the chest that human distress does.

The Hulk was already mostly formed and aggressively lurching towards our place in the entryway. The wailing was coming from further back in one of the corners.

Thankfully, there were no swirling shadows this time,

though the room was still ice cold and smelled of mossy stone and rain bouncing off heated iron.

"Well," I asked both Meghan and myself, "Now what?"

"It's time we earn our pay checks, Lair," she said, stepping forward and lighting a single candle in the darkness of the room.

"We aren't getting paid," I grumbled, pouring a thick pile of salt along the threshold to contain the conflict and give us a direction to escape when needed. I had no illusions that this might be resolved in a single knock-down drag-out. There were layers to this, so we were peeling an onion.

A cold, evil, noisy onion.

I briefly felt sorry for anyone staying in room 218 downstairs before throwing myself across the bed and into the far corner to lay down more perimeter salt.

The air in the back of the room was even colder than at the front door. My injured leg complained, but I started to walk the line of salt around the wall with the window. I felt the cold even in my relatively uninjured joints.

The wailing became an inhuman screeching that vibrated my eardrums and moved directly to my spine like a wet serpent made of ice.

Meghan took her own bag of salt and began pouring a circle

around herself, stealing furtive glances as the Hulk moved closer and closer to her kneeling form.

She began hastily setting out her stones and bowls and set her still-burning candle into one made of some silvery metal.

She shook her tiny brass bell, and the Hulk shuddered, horizontal lines of clarity shaking themselves through his stygian shape. His steps slowed and he actually began to lean back from the ringing sound.

I turned the corner and began to lay a line of salt around the wall that hosted the entrance to the bathroom, contorting myself to crawl under the desk and shoving the TV stand forward to make room for even more salt behind that.

My shoulder protested but it would have to take a number.

The Hulk was starting to move towards Meghan again, just as she was haltingly beginning some kind of chanting that I would never bother to identify.

As the dark shape began to press itself against the barrier of the circle of salt, Meghan again raised the tiny brass bell.

A harsh, cutting arctic wind blasted through the room, making the curtains billow, scattering the circle of salt into random dust, and freezing the clapper of the tiny bell to the side with an icy crackle.

Meghan dropped the now useless bell in silence and thrust her hand under her arm to warm her suddenly frost-burned fingers.

She looked terrified.

The Hulk lunged down for her; grim, implacable menace thick in the frigid air.

I smelled wood ash and animal fat rendered down to grease. And I could smell fear, but I think that was likely just ours.

Meghan raised her left arm in a last-ditch doomed attempt to ward off the towering entity leaning over her.

"Hey!" I yelled lamely. I needed to get its attention.

"Bobby!" The thing slowed again and turned in my direction, "You're about a hundred years past your checkout time, big guy. This isn't your room anymore."

The shape seemed to swell, inflating to a size that took up my entire field of vision. I could only vaguely see through it. I could just make out Meghan staggering upright and digging around for something. I could also see a dark, spidery form skittering across the ceiling, shreds of a long black dress hanging beneath her. Anne-Marie.

"Housekeeping needs the room, guys," I hoped Meghan could see me gesturing to the area above her head, but Bobby was becoming somehow thicker. I was losing sight of everything as he loomed over me. "They need to change the sheets and put out fresh towels- "

An enormous inky black backhand interrupted my speech when it hit me and knocked me across the desk and into a tangle of equipment straps and my own limbs. And it was cold. So cold I could imagine not only never being warm again but also never having been warm before. It was like a full-body ice cream headache.

Fighting the urge to curl into a ball and just expire, I struggled to get back on my feet as Bobby reached for me again.

"Anne-Marie!" I pointed at her, and Meghan gasped and turned to look at the long-limbed thing over her head.

Anne-Marie swiveled her neck bonelessly and gazed into me with pitch-black eyes.

She shrieked, and my joints all locked up. My heart stuttered. It was piercing, but somehow personally so. I was pinned against the back wall by it, my thoughts muddy as I tried to grasp at a plan.

Bobby swung another ghostly fist at me. Fully manifested, he was faster than we had gotten used to him being, and he caught me full in the chest, flinging me back into the far corner.

Breath freshly knocked out of me, I tried to see around Bobby to Meghan and the exit, but everything was dark.

"Bobby, buddy," I raised my arms placatingly, "Listen! Bro to bro, you can do better. I'm not saying you should've shot her, but she's definitely being a bitch about it."

A dark spectral leg came up between mine, but I managed to swivel so that he just clipped my hip. My injured hip.

It instantly went numb, and I pitched over onto the bed, kicking up the smell of dust and ancient mildew. The numbness was probably a mercy. At least it was as long as I could still move.

"Is that sexist, Meghan?" I asked, "When I called the demented lady ghost a bitch, did I cross a line?"

I scrambled across the bed I was on and onto the floor between it and the other one.

I could see her putting something into a tiny bowl on the ground, eyes locked on the ghost over her. Anne-Marie seemed to be watching me. I had the attention I'd been seeking.

Take that, high school guidance counselor.

Bobby lunged across the bed at me, and I ducked back towards the nightstand as I hoped Meghan had something amazing going in that bowl.

I jumped up, and squishily space walked across the second mattress and down to the floor again, leg aching.

I was between Meghan and the door, but I wasn't about to

leave her. I just had to trust that her plan was better than mine.

"Bobby," I waved at the huge form, making its more graceful way across the bed to follow me, "there have been a lot of changes over the past hundred years. Even though Anne-Marie is objectively being quite a bitch, we shouldn't just go around saying that."

Bobby slammed into me, freezing the breath in my lungs and knocking me back into the tiny bathroom. I slid across the tile and cracked my head on the bathtub.

"The disrespect, you see," I clambered to my feet again, "that's how you get people talking shit about you on Twitter."

Blackness filled the doorway. I was cornered. I couldn't go around him.

So I went through.

I led with a clenched fist full of salt, which I released inside the shadow itself, partially on purpose but mostly because my hand went numb from the cold almost instantly.

I fell through him and crashed back into the bed, slamming my forearm into the frame and whiplashing my head to the side.

Bobby was gone. Just gone.

Meghan was huddled over her bowl, struggling to set a pile of something inside it on fire as Anne-Marie extended a long, bony arm down towards her neck.

I stood up and swatted at the thing. You know, like someone without a plan or any common sense would do.

The cold was electric. My arm locked in place to the shoulder, and I struggled with the rest of me to pull back from the glacial pull of her.

Meghan stood, lifting the now smoldering bowl towards Anne-Marie.

"Get away from him," she intoned, "you bitch!"

Anne-Marie recoiled, and I fell to the floor.

Megan grabbed my still-numb arm and pulled me out the door and onto the too-familiar hallway carpet.

The door clicked shut again behind us.

"I know you were just quoting Sigourney Weaver," I said, "but with that language, you're still going to get canceled."

Chapter Thirty-Two

I had put a line of salt across the threshold of room 316, and Meghan and I huddled inside.

The warm burn of Irish copper pot distilling was putting some warmth back into my bones. Or at least I felt like it was. That's the important part, right?

"That was mostly sage," Meghan explained, "sage and cedar and mugwort to give it a little extra oomph."

"Mugwort," I took another drink, "just like mom used to make."

Meghan laughed. She had wrapped her frostbitten fingers in a warm washcloth and was scrolling through some notes on her phone.

"It's too much to ask for that to be the end of her, right?" I asked.

"Way too much," Meghan confirmed, "We took her by surprise tonight. It was a sucker punch, at best."

"My dad always said, 'If you have to fight, don't fight fair,'" I shrugged.

"Yeah," she acknowledged, "but we also bloodied the nose of her big gun, so next time, we have to expect your Hulk to come at us even harder."

I mentally cataloged my injuries.

My left knee and hip had taken some damage, and my right ankle was suffering from taking up the slack. My right shoulder was pretty messed up, and my left forearm was probably fractured.

I'd had an NFL training camp's worth of cranial trauma, including some you could still read across my forehead, even in low light.

I knew even without our hard stop on Sunday night, I wouldn't have it in me to take additional beatings anyway.

"We also managed to finally draw out Anne-Marie," she added, "I guess she had been hiding behind her swirl of ghosts before."

"So, how do we get rid of them both?" I was more than a bit foggy about the process of de-ghosting a place.

"I could give you some line about convincing them to go to the light or whatever," Meghan replied, "but that's barely an option."

"Thanks," I acknowledged, "Just so you know, I was prepared to go along with it. What can I say? Head injury," I gestured.

"We just need to de-escalate," she nodded, "I don't think

room 318 was dangerous before it got all stirred up by the local coven."

"I scrubbed Bobby's headstone clean today," I said, "not for any paranormal reason. I just felt someone needed to."

"You remember he was a pimp and a bootlegger, right?" Meghan asked.

"I've had bad days too," I explained, "Personally, I would hate to be defined by them."

"We may be able to use that," she said, "I think your words had an impact on him just now."

"If I get dragged on ghostly Instagram, that's fine," I allowed.

"You upset him," she stressed, "He's vulnerable when you malign his lady, Lair."

"She's totally malignable," I offered, "you know how when your friend breaks up with their significant other and you talk shit about them and then they get back together and then suddenly you're the asshole? It's been a century. He knows. We're cool."

"We need to scrub the back wall of the hotel," she suggested, "Breaking every connection is how we get this done."

"I can clean the wall tomorrow," I offered, "I've got a bunch of scrubby stuff left over from my visit to the cemetery."

"Do that," she ordered, "it can't hurt."

"We have one other thing on our to-do list," I lifted my dwindling whiskey.

"Yeah," she waved me off, "I know. Brunch."

The dreams always start the same way.

I'm on a quiet cul-de-sac, looking at the front of a comfortably worn house. Walking up the front steps I can't help but look up at the beadboard ceiling over the small front porch. It's covered in spiderwebs and abandoned wasp nests.

It's haint blue. It scatters spirits.

It's like the bright orange highway cone in front of the horrifically inebriated street racer.

Yeah, sure, it's a demarcation, but only for someone playing by the same rules as everyone else.

Inside, my cat is dead. She was almost eight years old and perfectly healthy, but that didn't matter.

She is curled up in the corner of the kitchen and stiff as a stone, her face frozen in an open-mouthed rictus and her tiny claws out as if to rend something that absolutely wouldn't feel threatened by that.

Something that's sitting on the corner of the kitchen island, swinging its legs and silently clapping its little red hands together.

Chapter Thirty-Three

Sunday brunch can, and should, be observed without getting thrown around by an angry ghost the night before. It's the most important made-up meal of the weekend in all circumstances.

It's just somehow better if you can contrast it with having been recently pitched into a bathtub. That's just culinary science.

I met Meghan a little before noon at The Cavalier, technically a bar, but a bar with a pretty popular brunch menu.

It's basically everything I like about being alive, so it was the perfect place to recover from an encounter with the dead. To feel human again.

It's vital to dress appropriately for brunch. Jeans and a worn flannel shirt over a t-shirt that read, "Have you tried turning it off and turning it back on again?" communicated my need for carbs and caffeine with simple elegance.

Meghan was wearing another dark flowing dress under yet another cardigan. She looked ready to shush someone for dragging a chair across the library floor, but it worked for brunch as well.

Breakfast tea steeped in a cup in front of her next to a pink grapefruit mimosa.

I had settled on a cup of coffee, which was rapidly cooling

since I'd found a brunch cocktail with Irish whiskey in it, and not drinking with brunch would undo all of the careful work I'd done selecting my outfit.

"Disrupting the spell is fine and all," Meghan sipped at her tea after blowing across the top, something I assumed tea drinkers do regardless of temperature, "but we need to knock Anne-Marie down a bit if we want her to revert to a harmless haunting."

"How do you de-escalate a ghost with a hundred years of anger issues?" I asked around my whiskey drink. The lemonade, black tea, and honey were interfering with the whiskey a bit too much for me, but I'm not really one to judge. Sometimes, I even resent ice cubes.

"You scrub the wall," she said, "I'll get some supplies from The Cauldron by the college."

"You shop there?" I don't know why I was surprised. There aren't exactly a lot of places in the southeast to pick up witchy stuff.

"I stop in from time to time," she smiled, "and I have a subscription to a few monthly herbs."

"Now you're talking like this is Colorado," I joked, "Have you ever run into a customer with lavender hair?"

I realized immediately that this wasn't anywhere near descriptive enough for the Austin underground.

"She's maybe five feet tall," I continued, "short, spiked hair."

"Madeline Murphy," she nodded, "She supplies a lot of the herbs and candles they sell there. They can charge a premium because she's a local."

"Is she," I struggled for a word, spinning a finger around my temple, "Touched?"

Meghan giggled, "She's a gifted medium. She doesn't do it professionally, but she has unsettled a bunch of people by being creepily personally accurate."

Our food arrived. Meghan had the chicken and waffles (a solid choice, if uninspired) while I had opted for the Build Your Own biscuits and gravy, which I ordered with a fried egg and avocado because if avocado is an option, you should always take it.

Avocados are a miracle.

They were the preferred food of the giant ground sloth in Central America before the last ice age, their enormous pits passing through the digestive tracts to be deposited in fresh, fertile soil somewhere else.

The sloths are extinct, so guacamole only exists due to the diligent agricultural work of our ancestors.

It would be disrespectful to the dead to not enjoy the

avocado.

"She said 'he' was chasing me," I explained, "but then she was a little surprised we were hunting a local ghost."

"Oh," she dragged part of a chicken tender through maple syrup and layered a jalapeno pepper on top of her fork, "Yeah, she's not wrong, Lair."

"What does that mean?" I asked. The biscuits and gravy were great, life-changing even, but I was bothered.

She hesitated, looking at me while arranging another bite of bliss on her fork, "Who hurt you, man?" She finally managed.

"I've seen some things," I started.

"I've seen things too," she interrupted, "This haunting is bad, yes, possibly the most dangerous I've seen," she took a sip of tea, "but the horrific things are just what we have to process, or we don't do this as long as you have."

The back of my throat felt desert dry. I took a sip of mostly lemonade and some merciful whiskey.

"I lived in a pretty haunted house a long time ago," I explained, "It wasn't as in-your-face as room 318, but it was harder not having another location to retreat to."

"How haunted?" She asked, eyes slightly narrowed.

"It was before I was in 'the life,' I guess, so the haunting scale is probably skewed."

"All haunting scales are skewed, Lair," she said, "you know that now."

"Now," I agreed, "but then? A million paranormal years ago? I was an idiot."

Meghan sighed, "My first experience was being visited by my grandmother," she said, "she just told me she loved me."

"Mine was spectral figures, dead pets, evil little monsters, and infestations of spiders," I explained.

"Spiders?" she asked.

"Yeah, like tens of thousands of brown recluse spiders living under the house," I nodded, "it was a whole thing. The breaker box in the garage was like Sandals Jamaica for spiders."

"Wait a minute," Meghan held up her hand, "South Carolina?"

"Yeah," I said, "Why?"

"The house that was checked out by a priest and a rabbi and like three paranormal crews?"

"And multiple electricians," I added, "They all suggested we just move away."

"Everyone knows that story," she said, "it's the holy grail of haunted houses. The internet is in agreement. We all want to investigate it."

"There are awful things in that house," I replied, "and they can stay there."

Something in my tone must have communicated more than I had intended because Meghan fell silent.

"I learned that a haunted house isn't a fun ride at an amusement park," I said, "and I learned that the photos taken mid-ride aren't the ones you put on your fridge."

"What else happened?"

"Electronics caught on fire," I said, "Monsters did their monstrous things, pretty standard stuff, really."

She looked at me. Through me. Into me.

"Madeline Murphy," she said, "Madeline Murphy could see it too."

I looked at the fluffy torn end of the waffle speared on her fork too intently.

"Are you telling me," I looked guiltily at my brunch drink, "something from that house is following me? All these years later?"

"It's years for you, sure," she said, "but years mean less to entities like that. Humans can hold grudges for decades. These things can be, and usually are, made of grudges."

"Hell, yeah, we can hold grudges!" I extended my hand across the table for a fist bump. A fist bump which was not returned.

"It's not the problem for tonight," she replied, "but it could be *a* problem for tonight."

"And we don't need any more of those," I agreed, "but there isn't anything I can do about that possible problem right now. So, what can we do?"

"Scrub the wall this afternoon," she advised, "and get some rest. Look for any sign that The Morrigan is still acting on the occupants of room 318."

"No problem," I replied, opening my wallet to pay the tab, "This showed up, by the way," showing her the black feather still tucked against my driver's license.

"Yeah," she sighed, "exactly like that."

"Maybe pick up a book of Celtic mythology for me at The Cauldron?" I asked, "I want something to read on the flight home."

"Good idea," she nodded.

Chapter Thirty-Four

I don't know if you've scrubbed clean an alley wall in Austin in the middle of the day, so I'll just say it isn't as glamorous as it sounds.

It was difficult to determine what the "paint" actually was, but it certainly wasn't off-the-shelf Sherwin Williams, and I couldn't easily tell, even in broad daylight, where it stopped and typical stained brick from behind the dumpster of an active kitchen began. When I say I'd rather be cleaning a headstone, I have recent experience with both and speak from authority.

I couldn't tell if our coven had returned the night before, but I really didn't think they had. We had probably terrified that lady. I felt a little bad about it, but on the other hand, she had literally asked for this by seeking some divine intervention in a matter that was pretty well settled a century ago.

I took the leftover soap and abrasives and brush and bucket and dropped them into the convenient dumpster before hopping the guard rail again and crossing the patio to the bar entrance.

I watched the shadows lengthen on 7th street behind the hotel, cars loaded with college students and business travelers taking advantage of the last gasp of the weekend before heading back to their familiar grinds on Monday, optimistically circling the area for a free parking spot. I didn't even live here, and I knew most of them would give up and drop fifteen bucks for a spot in an awkward improvised lot where they'd be advised to stow their valuables in the trunk or take them along on whatever adventure they would have that evening.

I slipped inside, picking up a glass of Irish whiskey over ice before heading back to the patio to watch the sun slip behind the buildings and the street fill with people with more standard plans to close out the weekend than I had. The pedal bars mostly stuck to the other side of the hotel on 6th street, but I watched one roll slowly past, filled with what I assumed was a bachelorette party.

A group of grackles, gray and black birds that compete with pigeons for urban garbage in this part of the world, picked at bits of a discarded soft pretzel on the sidewalk. They hypnotically darted about, grabbing bits of bread and flapping off again to the perimeter.

With a raspy chatter, a black bird with white markings on its breast and wings dove down into the middle of the flock and scattered them, tearing off a piece of street pretzel before jumping up onto the railing of the patio to consume her prize.

She shifted on the bar and fixed her gaze on me, tilting her head in that odd way birds do. She hopped from table to chair back to table over to where I was sitting, a wad of street pretzel still grasped in her black beak.

She (and I don't know why I called her "she"; I'm not an ornithologist) set down her stolen food and pinned it to the table with one taloned claw, watching me the entire time.

"I'm not going to steal your pretzel, lady," I assured her.

She seemed to nod quickly, then resumed picking apart her bit of pretzel.

"I've done worse at Oktoberfest," I offered, "There was spicy mustard involved, but that's not a brick I'm about to throw from this glass house."

She chattered again, a sound at once aggressive and yet somehow mimicking human laughter in some way.

I slowly waved my hands at her in what was an attempt at bird comfort and stood up, "Please," I said, "stay for a moment."

I walked to the back of the patio, keeping my eyes on her. She was watching me as well, between her attempts to dissect that pretzel. There was a large cooler with ice water and a stack of plastic cups, as well as some collapsible bowls for those people who bring their dogs to patio bars. I love those people. As long as their dogs aren't those constantly angry and very loud tiny dogs.

I poured a bowl full of cold water and returned to the table, slowly placing it in front of the bird.

She eyed it and me with a look I would classify as appraising.

She chattered at me again, more slowly than before. I got the impression she was speaking slowly, like clueless adults speak to children.

With a sudden burst of movement, she rocketed back to the sidewalk, scattering the grackles who had just returned to pillage the fallen pretzel again. She took a proud strut around the scene again before tearing off another piece and gracefully returning to place it in front of me.

"Oh, thanks," I chuckled, "but I'm not eating that."

She dipped her black beak into the water bowl and shook her head, then climbed in and splashed around a little. Whatever you can do to stay cool, I guess.

We continued to watch each other for a while. Her tiny body sloshed water out of the bowl and through the metal grate of the table onto the hot bricks of the patio. I stayed as still as possible, trying to process the life choices I had made that resulted in my setting up an improvised birdbath at a fancy hotel.

She abruptly jumped onto the edge of the plastic bowl and shook herself, methodically, beak to tail, spraying water onto the back and seat of the chair opposite me. She cocked her head at me again as if I hadn't moved. She hopped decisively towards me and plunged her face into my drink.

Before, I had been frozen in polite curiosity. Now, it was shock as I watched the level of Irish whiskey visibly drop in my glass.

She raised her head and stared at me for a moment before shaking herself off again and flying back to the sidewalk, where she almost casually plucked an eyeball out of the slowest grackle with her beak before spreading her wings and vanishing into the gathering Texas night.

Chapter Thirty-Five

An increasingly common side effect of having a touchscreen gateway to the total sum of human knowledge in our pockets is that any random new information can send us into a spiral down internet research rabbit holes. I'm certainly a victim. No joke, one time I realized at three in the morning that I'd been researching the Land of the Lost TV series from the 70's for six hours because a friend had sent me a meme.

Anyway, it turns out grackles are very common in Austin. The mockingbird may be the State Bird of Texas, but grackles are so common, in fact, that many consider them their unofficial City Bird of Austin. They stick to the edges between forest and farmland in rural areas, but here in the city, they congregate in huge plagues (seriously, that's the actual collective name) of hundreds of birds in city parks and parking lots, and instead of destroying crops, they pretty much eat garbage. They'll snatch the food right out of your hand. There's a place to leave them a review on Austin's Yelp page, but I doubt the grackles read it. Even the ones that still have both eyes are almost certainly illiterate.

Texas public education is in a rebuilding several decades.

For as much as they resemble crows, grackles are unrelated, having lighter and more iridescent feathers in the proper lighting, and if they happen to be free of the coating of bus exhaust that they tend to pick up living in the city. Like we all do.

Austin does have crows. The suburbs have encroached on the historical farmland where they live, and they've been encroaching back. They eat the eggs from backyard hipster chicken coops and have switched from stealing corn from a farmer's field to stealing corn chips from food bloggers.

Austin also has a recovering population of ravens, or, as the locals call them, "giant angry crows." They are one of the only birds or animal of any kind, including humans, willing to take on a Canadian goose while also being sober. And they are big, so while they undoubtedly grab the occasional unattended nacho, they also famously make off with spare change, wedding rings, and key fobs right off the valet podium. If it's shiny, it is to be coveted. Ravens are like people in that way.

The corvid that Austin doesn't have is the magpie, like the one that just bathed on my table and had shared my whiskey. Magpies also typically don't attack other birds. Sure, they generally don't have a fear of people, but they also don't prefer Irish whiskey to water, so this encounter wasn't just odd for me. It was the kind of thing that would leave David Attenborough speechless. The black-billed lady I'd shared my drink with wouldn't appear east of the Rocky Mountains, and she wouldn't be this far south.

Magpies, like other corvids, are smart birds. They remember specific people and form bonds with the ones they like. And grudges against the ones they don't. They can recognize themselves in a mirror, which is sometimes more than I can do in the morning.

They will also make off with shiny things, and apparently that includes coppery single-malt whiskey.

Opportunistic feeders, like their taxonomic cousins, magpies feed on the dead, often stealing meat from wolf kills. You can bet they shared a meal with the Donner Party.

In Europe, the magpie was maligned by the early church for being indifferent to the crucifixion, while the dove was somehow magically sad about it. Magpies were said to have a drop of the devil's blood in their tongue, which was the only thing preventing them from human speech. Countless birds were mutilated trying to test that theory. And in pre-Christian times the number of magpies that appeared at once was supposed to be prophetic.

One for sorrow

Two for joy

Three for a girl

Four for a boy

Five for silver

Six for gold

Seven for a secret never to be told.

A single magpie might be bad news, but I hadn't come away with that impression, really. She had been completely pleasant before the shocking violence at the end of our encounter. Let's just say I've definitely, and often, shared a drink with worse company.

The other thing about corvids is that we used to think they carried the souls of the dead to the other side, to the Ghost World or Valhalla or the Underworld. As such, the ancient Irish associated them with The Morrigan, the Chooser of the Slain. The Phantom Queen herself often appears in the form of a crow.

Chapter Thirty-Six

"What's up with the bird porn, Lair?" Meghan smirked over my shoulder.

"Don't kink shame me, Meghan," I replied, closing my laptop, "you missed a whole thing with a magpie stealing my whiskey."

"I'll take 'sentences no one has ever said before' for $1000, Alex." She riffed.

"Eh," I gestured vaguely around the patio, "you know how hotel bars are."

"Other than confirming that magpies are brave enough to get between you and your whiskey," Meghan asked, "did you learn anything useful?"

"Not anything I'm prepared to believe," I answered, "this bird had no reason to be anywhere near here other than the patio bricks are the same as the ones I had just scrubbed some pagan Celtic graffiti off of."

"Are you getting all witchy on me, Lair?" She playfully punched my uninjured shoulder, "Want me to consult your ancestors or fling some tarot for you?"

"No thanks, Meghan," I laughed, "I know my future, and I

don't want some cards rubbing it in."

She looked at me again in a way that reminded me of why I prefer to work alone.

"The back wall is clean," I changed the subject, "so I guess both ends of the ritual or whatever are closed off."

"So," she sat on the chair next to me that hadn't gotten bird water on it, "Anne-Marie should be at her normal activity level."

"If that's even what was juicing her up," I still wasn't quite convinced, but I didn't have anything better to cling to as a theory.

Meghan took a sip of something fizzy. Ginger ale, probably. I doubted she was ready for champagne this early.

"We still need to be ready," she said, "because we won't know until she *lets* us know."

"Pessimism or prophecy, Meghan?" I asked. "Either way, I'll take it."

"Something just isn't right about this," she considered, "she's had years and years to get angrier about her own murder or to get over it and cross over. Whatever ritual they've been doing has to be what's stirring her up, right?"

"I don't know," I answered, "there's betrayal all around this thing, but I'm thinking maybe we should lean into the canceled wedding angle tonight."

"Oh," she said wryly, "You're choosing the depressing angle? Color me shocked."

"I have a process," I waved, "if we work with the theory that some, if not most, particularly vicious hauntings involve spirits who may not know they've even died, the motivation is easier to understand."

"I'm sure she knows that she's dead," Meghan stated, "I can feel that. I can feel that she knows who killed her and that she's not at all okay with it."

"Details," I cut her off before this went full woo-woo, "it's not the death. It's the interruption of plans.

"Anne-Marie had plans, right? She was going to marry the love of her life in the finest venue in the city and then become a mother and a pillar of society here in Austin."

"And then she found out Bobby wasn't even proper boyfriend material, a pimp and a bootlegger and possibly a murderer," she nodded slowly, "so she decides to talk to the Feds, knowing it would blow all of that up."

"Decades before witness protection was a thing, too," I felt like I was on to something, "her whole life, or the plan for it, the direction she had chosen, was gone the second she decided to call the FBI."

"And almost immediately interrupted," Meghan finished, "That's enough to strand anyone in a timeless kind of over-and-over misery of repetition."

"It's like working a help desk," I sagged, "but eternal."

She playfully punched my shoulder again, but I had actually been sincere in my commiseration. We use our plans to define ourselves. We set goals for ourselves. We have expectations for the way our lives are going to go. Trajectories even.

It's physics.

I've been working around computers for longer than I'd like to admit, and I've never met a single person who said they'd like to spend their days talking to someone who makes eight times more than they do through saving a PDF.

When it comes down to it, we all do whatever it is we do to survive. It's another one of those unavoidable DNA-level imperatives.

A little kindness goes a long way. The same rules apply to our interactions with the dead, usually.

Usually.

But we were in a bit of a time crunch. It was our turn to escalate.

"We need to ramp up the emotion," I decided, "we force her

to face the world as it is instead of the way she had planned."

"And how exactly," she asked, "do we manage that?"

"For starters," I tipped my suddenly and mysteriously empty glass at her, "I am going to crash a wedding."

Chapter Thirty-Seven

The Hendricks-Wasserman wedding reception in the first-floor ballroom, a rare Sunday night wedding, was an understated affair, especially for The Fountain House LLC.

Nonetheless, I was NOT dressed for the affair. I was wearing black cargo pants, pockets stuffed by habit with EMF detectors, digital voice recorders, a laser thermometer, and a pocketful of salt for some future emergency.

I was also wearing my black cowboy boots and a t-shirt that featured a bearded man in robes and sandals with a broom that read "Jesus swept."

All of us are going to eventually die. When it is my turn, I intend to deserve it.

Thunder rumbled in the dark sky outside, so this wedding was probably a disappointment for the happy couple already. Getting hitched in an antique rooftop garden sounds nice. I just hoped the weather didn't chase everyone back down here early.

With a half-apologetic shrug, I pushed my way into the ballroom and edged toward the tables lined up on the far side of the room. I stole a silver gift bag, slid the coffee maker out, and stuck the tag from the bag directly onto the top of the box.

I grabbed a couple of fancy commemorative wedding programs and some monogrammed paper napkins and started looking around for anything that made me think, "You have to waste hours of your life at a wedding."

I took a little mesh bag of birdseed. Then I turned back and took a second bag because maybe I'd need birdseed.

I tossed in a few of those weird powdery cookies I only ever see at weddings and glanced back at the door before ducking behind the modest but still oversized, going by the number of tables, wedding cake.

Continuing to hack away at whatever karmic goodwill the universe may have ever had for me, I cut a decent-sized piece of cake off the very back, slapped it onto a plastic plate, and set it carefully in the bag along with the rest of my pilfered wedding swag.

I took a few disposable forks and made my way to the exit, pausing only to snag a small vase of flowers right by the door before slipping to the stairwell and up to my room to stash everything.

"I have raided a wedding," I announced as I slid back into my chair on the bar patio next to Meghan with a fresh drink, "The ghostly emotional gut punch is on deck and waiting for us to nerve up and get to it."

"You're going to hell for that, Lair," she advised.

"I mean, obviously," I admitted, "but probably not for *that*."

"So, what would it take for you to just stay?" She asked.

Meghan seemed pensive. Less let's-go-bust-some-ghosts and more let's-flood-the-comments-section-on-The-View.

I looked at her, puzzled, "I guess you don't mean Austin. Like I shuffle off my mortal coil and just hang out?"

"Yeah," I noticed she had switched up to cola and something in a rocks glass. This was probably alcohol-fueled seriousness, "Why would *you* haunt a place?"

I considered it. It was a pretty heavy question for a patio conversation.

"Meghan," I offered, "I don't care at all about my finished business, so I can't imagine my unfinished keeping me tethered to anything."

Fat raindrops slapped the pavement. Rain in central Texas is brief but heavy. It leads to flooding sometimes, but mostly because we are still somehow completely unprepared for it.

"We stay for love, Lair," she said, "we do everything for love because we are idiots."

I'm never going to be someone who argues that we somehow aren't idiots. I've met people. You've met people.

It's objectively true.

"So, you'd stay," I grinned, astounded, "you'd just hang out all corpsified and angry?"

"If I had an agenda," she said, "I would absolutely follow it. I don't like leaving things to do."

I tipped my glass at her.

"Congratulations for giving a shit," I offered, "I award you no points, but they sold a plastic tiara at that general store, and I will happily pony up the cash for that."

"Love, Lair," she smiled back at me sadly, "Love is the basis of justice, and justice is how we find peace."

Chapter Thirty-Eight

"That is a hideous handful of wedding cake you've got there," Meghan said.

"I know. I was in a hurry, okay?" I was trying to make it look as nice as possible on the plate again, "At least that couple has 'something borrowed' covered, right?"

"You know this isn't how that works," she smirked, "but we are far enough off script at this point that worrying about details would be a waste of time."

"What is our plan tonight?" I asked, "I'd like to vote against me vaulting across the room to pour salt along the baseboards. Because I feel like that was wildly unpopular last time."

"Yeah, obviously," she agreed, "you lay out the wedding stuff while I arrange the ritual work."

"Do I need details on this ritual?" I asked.

"Would it matter? Would you listen?"

"I'm missing context, sure," I admitted, "what about nuance?"

She arched an eyebrow at me, "You're allergic to nuance."

"I'm allergic to fresh-cut grass, Meghan, I love nuance."

"How did you play soccer as a kid?"

"Very poorly, but for a variety of reasons."

"The ritual itself is simple," she explained, "I'm going to cast a circle and invite the spirits to cross over."

"We've done that before," I said, "how is this different?"

"It's different because you," she pointed, "will be ramping up the emotional energy with this wedding stuff you pilfered."

"Liberated," I corrected.

"Fine." She mocked, "Liberated. You just talk up the wedding and marriage and life plan junk. Worst case, it distracts them while I do my thing."

"Best case, they immediately decide to honeymoon on some remote mesa in Mexico."

"I doubt you will be able to gaslight the ghosts into moving to Mexico, Lair."

"Actually," I smiled at her, "the proper term is 'gas-lamping.'"

She wisely chose to ignore me.

"If Bobby was going to call off the wedding for infidelity or because he knew she was working with the Feds," Meghan said, "then he's only sticking around because Anne-Marie has trapped him here. You get her focused on her unfinished business, and maybe he can get free of her.”

“Then we pack up, check out, and grab a final victory brunch in the morning,” I added, “this sounds like an excellent plan.”

Chapter Thirty-Nine

This was a terrible plan, I thought as I hastily arranged the programs and flowers around the admittedly terrible slice, or technically wad, of cake on the desk in room 318.

The temperature had dropped instantly in the room as soon as we opened the door, and it was growing colder as I worked.

Meghan was arranging her bowls and stones and herbs in the middle of the room around a circle of salt between the two beds. She was murmuring too softly for me to make out individual words. Much like the whispers filling the darkness around us.

Lightning cracked across the sky, and sharp thunder rattled the glass in the window frame. The smell of ozone washed over us, adding a layer to the scent of drying cake and dying flowers, which had been unable to overcome the room's smell of wet ashes.

A low growl shook the floorboards from the corner of the room as the too-familiar dark, hulking shape began to coalesce.

"It's time to get this relationship back on track," I announced to the room, "start acting like the happy couple you should have always been!"

A cackle of high-pitched laughter echoed from the ceiling. I couldn't see anything there, but I had the feeling something could see me.

"We are gathered here today," I began, "to celebrate a special, timeless, eternal kind of love." I gestured at the desk, "Please, have some cake!"

Wind howled outside the window, and more fat raindrops battered at the glass. Lightning flickered in the night sky and a continuous peal of thunder made me lose track of the growling shape making its way toward me. Bobby was getting quicker about manifesting. Practice makes horrific, I guess.

With a bony shriek, Anne-Marie dropped from the ceiling over the bed nearest the door and scuttled under the box spring. I moved to put myself between Meghan and the bed and waited for a skeletal hand to grab my ankle. Coils of shadow squirmed from under the bed like some prehistorically massive octopus. Sometimes, the monster under the bed is real. And angry.

"As a member of the clergy," I started again, "duly ordained by a totally real internet church, I am here to officially wed you two crazy kids."

I danced back as one of the tendrils of shadow brushed against my foot, instantly chilling me through my boot. It was cold enough to make me think of those people who lose toes in documentaries about mountain climbing.

Meghan continued her indistinct chanting, but a glance told me her eyes were open. She hadn't moved. She was trusting me to keep her safe.

"Do you, Bobby, take this ghastly abomination under the bed to be your wife, in life and in death, forever and ever, in this tiny, outdated hotel room?"

The shape lunged at me, one inky arm passing through my chest and tossing me onto the bed. Directly over Anne-Marie.

Icy tentacles thrust through the mattress and pinned my arms to my chest, my lungs crackling from either the pressure or the cold. I attempted to twist in place, but it was futile.

My vision began to blacken at the edges as I struggled to draw breath. I kicked with my legs until they too were wrapped up and stuck to the mouldy ancient mattress.

My struggle became weaker as I was pulled downward, more token twitching than anything else.

I gasped and was startled to hear the finality of it.

The darkness became total.

The dream didn't start the same way.

I was in bed in the bedroom of a comfortably worn house

next to a golf course that I'd never visited.

I felt I needed to sleep, but I couldn't. I knew I couldn't, and I also knew that my trying to sleep, the urgency, was only adding to the cumulative exhaustion of years of interrupted sleep and lack of any measure of meaningful rest.

Familiar shadows floated around the bed, but those didn't bother me anymore. It was the tapping.

TICK TICK TICK – Sharply in the dark. Like it was demanding my attention.

TICK TICK TICK – Not steady, not rhythmic. Insisting I hear it.

TICK TICK TICK – What the hell was it?

Something scampered up onto the bed and across me. Some THING.

It pressed itself against my face and began to smother me into my sweat-soaked pillow. I couldn't breathe, but honestly, I wasn't sure I wanted to, anyway.

I was too tired. Too scared. Too late. Too done.

I did the stupid thing.

I fought back.

I beat it.

I survived it.

And then?

Then I lost.

Chapter Forty

With a scream, I tore myself through the apparition trying to squeeze me to death, frozen cords in turn tearing insubstantially but painfully through my bones and organs, leaving an ache that felt soul-deep.

I rolled off the bed and onto the floor, looking directly into the stretched skin of Anne-Marie's grinning rictus under the bed.

She shrieked again – That cry that cut through skin and went directly to bone.

Meghan was still doing her thing, kneeling on the dim carpet and invoking whatever. She faintly glowed with some inner light, which was mirrored in Anne-Marie's skittering form. This ritual was somehow working on both of them, intentionally or not. Syllable by syllable, it was doing whatever it did to Meghan at the same time as Anne-Marie.

I hadn't been gone for too long. I could still do something.

Lightning speared the clouds again as the storm outside intensified. The thunder shook the window and my spine at the same time.

Black wings painted themselves in shadow across the back wall of the room as the whispers began to announce their purposes.

"Another soul."

"Fresh memories."

"Not him."

"He's still broken."

"He's company?"

"He. Brought. Us. A. Wedding."

"We keep him."

The Hulk was leaning over towards Meghan again, so I mentally thumbed through my suddenly pathetically minimal toolkit and settled on the old standard.

"Damn it," I muttered, flinging myself into the air and into the Hulk again.

The cold was shocking in the strobing illumination of the lightning, but as my salt-filled vest pocket passed through Bobby, he became insubstantial again, and I bounced off the far mattress and onto the floor.

"Dammit. Bobby." I Hank Hill'd face down into the ancient woolen carpet.

Meghan stood, holding up brass censors of incense in each hand, her voice raising into a wordless crescendo as Anne-Marie retreated towards the headboard, still skittering obscenely under the bed.

I struggled back to my feet, every joint complaining about my decision-making process over the past week. Or for the past several years. They weren't wrong but this was not the time for me to be doing that math.

Dark tendrils of shadow were making their way around the room, scattering random objects in the bathroom, my long-dead equipment, and that heavy ashtray again. They were also casting harsh shadows in the lightning-lit room.

Bobby began the process of re-forming in the doorway to the tiny bathroom. When he finished, he would be a single step away from being between the two of us and the room's only exit. I didn't enjoy the thought of going through him again. I was slowing down already. Another trip through the dead, and I wasn't sure I'd be standing right back up again. If I ever did.

"Do I hear wedding bells?" I asked, ringing my tiny brass bell as hard as I could, the chimes rebounding off the dark walls and each note vibrating the Hulk violently, "A hundred years isn't too late!"

Meghan was still at it, waving her sacred smoke around the room as the scuttling thing under the bed began keening in response.

"So, Bobby," I asked, "are you guys going to have kids right away, or are you going to wait?"

A tentacle snaked around my ankle and announced that Anne-Marie no longer found me charming and clever. My leg numbed again from the cold, so I didn't really feel it when I was pulled off my feet, was slammed again into the carpet, and started getting dragged under the bed. I dropped the bell, and it rolled away.

I caught the bed frame with my other foot and attempted to pull myself free, but my trapped leg wouldn't respond to my very reasonable suggestion that it fight back as well. As numb as I was, I felt it when something began to chew on my calf.

Rotten, broken teeth ripped into the black denim of my jeans and began to worry away at flesh. I was close enough to see whatever Anne-Marie had become hunched over my frozen limb. She looked nearly feral, like some kind of grave-rotted monster. She looked solid.

I took a chance. She was less than twelve inches from a major artery, and I knew if she tore into that, I would bleed out in minutes.

In desperation and more terror than I'd like to admit, I let my good foot slip off the bed frame, and I kicked Anne-Marie in the face.

She did not like that, but she stopped chewing long enough

to shriek at me. I let the cry propel me out from under the bed, and I struggled to stand again, feeling hot wetness start to soak my sock and fill my boot.

I knew it was bad, but Meghan was still busy, and Anne-Marie had absolutely lost her ghostly shit.

She skittered up the far wall and across the ceiling again, crab-like, her eyes burning into mine. I've seen murderous looks before, but mostly from software sales reps.

Anne-Marie intended to end me and probably keep me forever in this awful hotel room. I'd be just another tool she would use to torment the living. Not only would I fail in my original mission, I would be making things worse. Possibly forever.

This room didn't even have a decent Wi-Fi signal or free HBO.

I flung salt at her and then a bundle of herbs Meghan had armed me with. Then I threw a handful of leaves of some sort I'd bought at the witchy store.

She didn't stop coming, but she slowed down, and her shrieking became a chittering sound, like bone on bone. Like a colony of ants inside my skull devouring each other and everything around them.

I couldn't hear Meghan anymore, but her lips still moved,

and her eyes were fixed somewhere far beyond the walls of room 318.

Lightning painted the sky a brilliant white, momentarily rendering me blind in the low light of the hotel room.

Momentarily, but long enough for the Hulk to slam into my back and knock me sprawling to the floor again.

Anne-Marie chose that moment to pounce, flinging herself towards Meghan as I struggled to get to my feet again.

I staggered in front of her, feeling icicle arms pass through my torso. My lungs froze in my chest, and I fell to my knees, but at least I kept her away from Meghan – who did not pause her ritual for a heartbeat.

Meghan's eyes snapped into focus. She began to produce new, weird bundles of herbs, handfuls of stones, and strange powders, which she was flinging with reckless but targeted abandon.

Her chant didn't waver for a second.

Anne-Marie went into a spectral frenzy, shadows slamming with whispery thuds into the walls, floor, and ceiling while she writhed in the center of the room, screeching in pained rage and flickering in and out of our vision. Or in and out of reality.

The Hulk slammed into me again, forcing me down to my side as my brain spun around itself, ideas completely out of stock but bloody, horrific visions available a bargain basement rates.

I hit him with a bag of birdseed, and he vanished – the wedding was over, I guess. The groom was dismissed.

With an unearthly POP, actinic light blasted the room. Electric cables in the walls burned through their sheetrock coverings around the baseboards and blew voltage out of outlet after outlet.

Sparks showered onto the carpet, and the smell of smoke began to obscure the less natural scents in the room. Lightbulbs exploded with the sound of gunshot glass, and a haze clouded room 318 worse than any of the incense we had deployed so far.

The bedside lamp began to hum ominously, sparks arcing across the exposed filament, and I couldn't look away from it. Or move. I was hypnotized, frozen by fear of the inevitable.

This ghost hunt had gone poorly, and I figured it was the last I'd ever be on, so that was appropriate.

Anne-Marie cackled again and extended an arm towards me, blue-white arcs of energy circling it as she gazed into me.

She drew back and pitched a ball of lightning at me as the sky echoed her rage, and I knew at the core of my being that this was over. I was done. Room 318 had been beyond my capabilities. I was dead, and I deserved it for any number of reasons.

Meghan calmly stepped in front of me. The bright ball of

electricity hit her in the chest, and she collapsed to the floor before me with a hole burned through her shirt and a charred, smoking hole in her torso.

She twitched twice, and I knelt next to her, hopeful that there was something I could do, that she might still be alive.

She did not move again.

Chapter Forty-One

The room fell silent. All the screeching and howling just stopped and I was left instead with an aching absence of sound.

Even the storm that had been battering the window had faded to a low patter.

I knelt and pressed a hand to the soft skin of Meghan's throat. There was no pulse.

I wanted to attempt CPR, but how would compressions work around a gaping hole in the sternum? I wanted to call 911 but my phone was a glossy glass-faced brick and had been since the first manifestation.

The carpet had blackened in several places, but it hadn't caught fire. The burns around the walls hadn't ignited either. Small favors, I suppose.

The activity had stopped in the room.

The silence burned in my ears. I knew there was something I needed to be doing but couldn't think of what it was.

I wanted to sit down next to Meghan and keep her company, but that didn't feel productive, so I walked back to room 316 and called 911. I reported a death in room 318 and requested assistance. I could hear my own voice, but I didn't recognize it. I identified myself and told the operator I would be waiting downstairs for the police or the paramedics or whoever would be coming.

She asked if I was in danger, and I told her I honestly didn't know and then I just hung up.

It is possible to know that you are in shock when you're in it, and it's also possible to know exactly what you can do about it, which in my case was nothing.

My partner, my friend, was dead in the next room because I had let her help me try to unravel the haunting in room 318. Because she had stepped in front of a paranormal hostility meant for me.

I looked at the bottle of whiskey on the nightstand and didn't want a drink. That probably meant something.

I took the stairs down to the lobby and stared at the revolving door as if I could will someone to appear who could help. Someone who could do anything at all.

My hands shook with a cold shiver that infected every part of me. It's just that my hands didn't have the responsibility of keeping me upright, so they got to indulge in it.

I started to see the red and blue flickering of emergency lights paint the rain-slicked windows and grow brighter before my eyes started to lose focus.

Focus which returned instantly when the whooping sound of

a fire alarm went off from the alley side of the building.

I knew what was on fire, and I knew it was a hell of a lot more flammable than the moldy carpet and drywall in room 318.

Charging the panicked night clerk, I dodged around the front desk and unclipped the fire extinguisher from the back wall before ducking past the small break room and into the storage room, which was piled floor to ceiling with stacks of chairs and tables. Most smoldered, and some already burned while Anne-Marie hovered in the middle of the room, pulling electricity out of the walls and into her dark tendrils of shadow.

I pulled the pin from the fire extinguisher like a grenade and began to spray piles of powder on everything, starting with the things actively on fire.

Anne-Marie shrieked and flickered in and out of vision as I darted around her, all my hope resting in a thick coating of fire suppression, keeping more fires from starting behind me.

The acrid smoke from burning foam and polyester was dense enough that I could no longer see the door I had come in from, but I could see the giant square of the garage door shut against the alley.

Electricity continued to arc across the room behind me as I struggled to find the mechanism to open the rolling door and release some of the smoke so I could see clearly. And also so I could breathe freely, which was fast becoming an issue.

The chain for the garage door ended in some kind of motor in a casing, so I looked around the walls for a button to raise it. My visibility was so low I had to move closely along the wall, navigating my way around stacks of still-smoking furniture.

I spotted two over-and-under, palm-sized buttons like they have on the podiums on Jeopardy, and I slapped the top button as quickly and as hard as I could, yelling, in a terrible Scottish brogue, "That's just how your mother likes it, Trebek!"

Nothing happened.

Nothing happened with the door, anyway. It just sat there, closed, like some kind of big, flat, aluminum jerk.

Sparks flew behind me and hissed into the walls and concrete floor. They didn't gain purchase in the remaining upholstered kindling in the room thanks to the coating of baking soda or whatever non-flammable dust I'd scattered around the room.

I idly considered that salt might work as a fire suppressant, too, and I resolved to buy another twenty-five pounds if I survived and if I ever wanted to do this again for some stupid reason.

It's funny what you think about when you're so close to death. Not like funny "ha-ha", but funny like "this-is-uncomfortable-to-think-about-and-look-at-where-thinking-got-us-anyway-smart-guy."

Anne-Marie raged on in the center of the room, her attempted arson becoming increasingly obvious in its futility. Shadows writhed around her dark form, agitated and twitching.

I worried that until she stopped sucking power out of the walls, getting the garage door open was a lost cause. Or, possibly, the wires to the open button had been melted inside the walls. The ventilation was only pushing the thick haze around the storage room. I still couldn't see the exit to the break room, and my lungs burned.

I took a quick inventory of my various injuries, which felt a bit like waking up most days.

My left leg was only holding me up anymore out of habit and grim determination, my right elbow and ankle were complaining about their forced participation in this whole adventure, my face still hurt from the ashtray incident and fresh carpet burn, my oxygen-starved lungs growled in my chest and, most pointedly, my heart ached.

It hurt like a cold hollow had been brutally carved out of the center of my chest like the divot in front of Bobby Rose's grave transplanted to my rib cage and filled with permafrost.

It should have been me, I thought. I had no right to be here, still breathing, however poorly I was doing it. This was my fault, my mess, my responsibility, *it should have been me.*

Anne-Marie decided to focus her rage on me. I deserved it. She objectively wasn't wrong.

She flickered and stuttered her way towards me, as angry as a freshly kicked mound of fire ants.

But fire ants are not native to Texas, and neither are ghosts, in my expert opinion. Plus, lighter fluid and grey market Mexican fireworks can only do so much about fire ants, however dramatic that effort may be.

Not for the first time, I decided my arsenal of anti-paranormal tricks was the equivalent of grey market fireworks and lighter fluid in a burning room.

Black tendrils of shadow wrapped their way around my legs, arms and neck, and I started to consider my own mortality again as black spots began to bloom across my vision.

She moved closer to me, gathering another deadly softball of electricity between her hands and rolling it around menacingly as she hovered between me and the large, immobile garage door.

I hacked and coughed violently, thick, black fluid running down my chin and chest as my lungs protested the abuse I had inflicted on them. Frantically, desperately, I sucked in more smoke-filled air, eyes darting about, trying to find something to duck behind that wouldn't just get burned through when that lightning came for me.

Hopelessness is its own kind of certainty. You can just know, heartbeat to heartbreak, that whatever you do, you will fail. It is as liberating as it is chilling.

I thought of John Cleese saying, "I can take the despair. It's the hope I can't stand."

When you are miles outside whatever passes for your comfort zone already and physically and emotionally battered, it is so simple to just sit down and wait for the inevitable unpleasant results of your choices. But just because something is simple doesn't mean it's easy.

I swung the empty fire extinguisher with the hose and advanced on the shuddering spirit that was all that remained of Anne-Marie, whipping it faster and faster in a circle and trying not to knock myself in the back of the head with it.

Before I could connect with a targeted swing, something grabbed my arms and lifted me a couple of feet in the air. Something huge. Bobby had returned.

I tried to struggle free, but I was pinned in place as Bobby began to move me, slowly at first but quickly accelerating until he slammed me face-first into the far wall.

I fell behind a smoking stack of folding tables and scrambled to stand on the slick concrete floor. Bobby had maneuvered himself between me and the exit to the lobby. There was no way I would make it through him fast enough to not give him several opportunities to attack or even kill me, and I didn't have the strength to force my way through him slowly either.

Anne-Marie was floating in front of the large rolling garage door as if that would be opening any time soon to provide an exit for me and all the smoke in the room. She still bounced a bright blue ball of sparks between her hands, her head twitching as if only vaguely connected to her neck. She cackled again, her mouth thrown open so wide I could almost count her too-many, jagged, broken teeth. She drew back an arm to pitch the ball of lightning at me, to burn a hole in my chest and commit her second murder of the evening.

I will admit my vision was clouded by a thick haze of smoke and my own lack of oxygen. Further, I was in a pretty fair amount of physical pain and emotional distress. It was dark, and I was already seeing things that would get me sent to the Grippy Socks Hotel if I had been telling them to a mandatory reporter.

So, when I tell you that Meghan appeared in the room with us, I understand if you take that with a twenty-five-pound bucket of driveway salt.

She was wearing the same chunky-knitted sweater and flowing dress she had been wearing when she first attached herself to this investigation, and she looked every bit as substantial as she always had.

And she glowed with that strange inner light I'd seen during her last invocation in room 318, reflected once again in Anne-Marie's shrieking form.

There was still a smoking hole in her chest.

She gave me a small, sad smile, rolled her eyes ruefully, and said, "The classics, right?" She tackled Anne-Marie, causing both of them to pass insubstantially through the closed aluminum garage door and out into the dark, rainy alley, knocking her off the grounds of The Fountain House Hotel and severing her connection to the sad place where she had died.

Bobby howled and followed after them like a cold, foul wind. Whether he did it on purpose or not, I couldn't say.

Chapter Forty-Two

The electrical chaos ended instantly, and the garage door began to roll open on its own, smoky air sucked out into the lightly rainy Texas night.

I staggered to the opening and breathed the first clean air I had tasted in what felt like forever. I was surprised that something that smelled so much like wet garbage could be an improvement on anything, but it felt like walking through a spring garden to me.

Anne-Marie and Bobby were nowhere to be seen. Neither was Meghan.

I guess she had unfinished business, and now that was complete. I wished the three of them peace and sat heavily on the edge of the loading dock. The first responders would be here any minute, and I would have questions to answer. Probably a lot of questions, as I was the only person with a key to the room where Meghan died, and I had inserted myself into a storage room fire at the same hotel right after.

I could hear booted feet stomping around in the lobby and stood to add my own to the noise.

I passed two firefighters on my way out of the room. They nodded at me after seeing my condition and the empty fire extinguisher on the floor. There would be follow-up questions, but

I was free to pass into the lobby to manage the Meghan . . . situation.

I approached two Austin night shift detectives and identified myself as the person who had made the 911 call, and explained what Meghan and I were doing in the hotel room. Or rather I explained that we were doing research on the hotel to help with marketing materials, which was true, technically. And technically true is the best kind of true.

They asked if I owned a heavily modified taser or stun gun, and I said I did not and added that I didn't think either stun guns or tasers worked like that.

They shrugged at each other and scribbled more notes on tiny pads. They took down my contact information and even tried to check if my phone rang when they dialed it, but it was still very dead.

Like Meghan, I thought, as the Medical Examiner's van pulled up by the valet parking podium. *It should have been me.*

A cloud of coroners hustled past me, without a glance, up the stairs to examine the body. They would return about an hour later with a body in a black vinyl bag on a stretcher, shuttling it past me and into the van to drive away for further examination.

By that time, I had told the story of our evening in room 318 about a dozen times. I had pictures from earlier visits up in room

316 but everyone wanted to know about this particular evening, for which I could only provide a narrative.

Gloria Anderson arrived, a little man with a briefcase trailing along behind her. I assumed he was an attorney.

She confirmed that Meghan and I had been contracted by the hotel to help out with marketing around the history of the place, with research into the stories told about it and a "review" of the most famous room.

When the press began to trickle in, the little man pivoted and insisted that all questions go through him. He refused to identify the victim or the only witness (which was me, and I appreciated that) and insisted on framing the whole incident as an unfortunate accident.

I heard him say it several times before the building high-pitched tone in my brain drowned out everything, including most of my thoughts. Most, but not all.

It should have been me. It was supposed to be me.

I think I got asked more questions eventually. As the sun started to paint the surrounding building with golden light, I sat in a chair in the lobby and considered fetching my things from room 316 and heading to the airport to pick a flight home. Room 316 seemed too far away for that plan to be practical.

Gloria had left with my report. Room 318 was still haunted by the sad but harmless Judith Mounier. The child ghosts would eventually return to the hallway. I recommended that future paranormal enthusiasts bring simple toys to offer them. It could be weeks or months or even years before they returned, but they would be back, I was certain.

She said she was sorry for what had happened to Meghan, and I had agreed. Several weeks later, we would get the official report from the coroner. Meghan had died when a freak bolt of lightning had arced through the room on the way to fry a vintage television. It was a one-in-a-million chance, but absolutely the only thing that made sense.

The hotel's insurance even paid out for the room to be renovated because it was considered an "Act of God," which is overall a terrible thing to say about a deity.

The room was safe to rent out to ghost hunters of any experience level. Mission accomplished in a way that left me entirely hollowed out and unable to even unpack and clean my ghost-hunting equipment.

What I had done was I immediately pulled the heavy glass ashtray out of my carry-on bag when I got home and rested it, quite harmlessly, on the mantle over the tiny fireplace in my loft.

I set the little statuette of The Morrigan next to it, her wings casting a shadow against the wall.

My cat, Aengus, disdainfully considered this haul further evidence of the pointlessness of my wandering and of my inadequate hunting skills. At the best of times, he's a difficult guy to impress, and I'm sure I was bad company after getting home, still reeling from the pain and the loss and noticeably limping.

I'd stared at my reflection in the glass for several minutes before finally uttering, "It should have been me that died."

Fingernails dug into the meat of my brain immediately, along with the heavily accented feminine croak of, "Ye are not th' one who chooses, Milesian. If the slain don' stay dead, ye bury 'em better an' deeper. Dat's yer role, ye scuttered feck. Nár chuire Dia ar do leas thú."

Epilogue

The dream was different again this time.

I am in a grassy field behind an old farmhouse, sheep wandering past an open gate to get to the better grass, which looks to me exactly like all the grass I can see.

A triangle-shaped opening in the earth under a hawthorn tree sits in the ground in front of me. It doesn't exactly invite me in, but even my dream self knows my going in is inevitable.

I crawl into the muddy hole in the ground, passing the Ogham script carved into the lintel over the entrance and down, down into the earth.

A ninety-degree turn down and to the left pulls me further into darkness so complete that I start to forget what seeing things is like.

The water dripping through the earth to plink against the stones around me is the sole sound in the darkness. It surrounds me. It embraces me.

Wet and caked in mud, cold and blind, I feel at home.

At the far side of the cavern, little reddish creatures invisibly hop from foot to foot and cackle soundlessly, making plans of their own.

"Nár chuire Dia ar do leas thú."

Irish for "May God never grant you peace".

Notes

This is a work of fiction. Any similarity to actual people, living or dead or undead is purely coincidental (and would actually be kind of cool).

What isn't fictional is most of the locations in this book. And, more importantly, the brunches. If you are going to be completely accurate about anything, that thing should be brunch. I've been to the restaurants and venues described on visits to Austin and if you're planning a trip for business, vacation or to poke at dead things, you could do way worse than to visit the places where these particular ghost hunters chose to eat.

The Fountain House Hotel is mostly fictional, a blend of two separate Texas haunted hotels which I've stayed in and investigated.

The side plot ghost stories from around Texas are part of the official local folklore and can be easily researched if you want to know more.

If you have the opportunity to take a ghost tour or enjoy a haunted pub crawl, please remember these are opportunities to embrace the local history, good and bad, and that's as true in Austin as it is anywhere else.

Only ghost hunt in structurally sound places and with the invitation of the legal owner of the property. Make sure your tetanus shot is up to date, too. It could save you some time later.

About The Author

Garrick is an IT security consultant and pub trivia monster. He owes this book to his friends and cheering section, Lilah, Kirsten, Joe, Natalie and Shipper, his mom and dad and his niece Kaleigh, the Keeper of the Drafts, and to his long-suffering roommates and cats, The Captain and Oberon.

He'd like to thank a few local Houston pubs where he almost entirely wrote this book, The Penny Whistle, On The Kirb, BB's and The Maple Leaf, 75% of which stock his favourite whiskey even though he's the only one who drinks it around here. He currently resides in midtown Houston over an abandoned and probably haunted grocery store, itself probably infested with ghoulies and ghosties and long-legged beasties.

Stalk him at your own risk.